HYSTERICAL FOR HARVARD

A JAKE LOGAN PRIVATE TUTOR MYSTERY

J.A. JERNAY

PLOTWORKS PUBLISHING

ONE

Acting is probably the most unstable profession in the world, and somewhere around my twenty-eighth birthday, I realized that my luck had finally run out.

After almost a decade of steady work that paid the bills, I hadn't gotten a part in six months. I hadn't even gotten an audition in three. So the result was inevitable.

I'd become a waiter.

My new workplace was the Earthen Jug, an unbearably trendy patio café in Santa Monica. Most of my time was spent slinging low-carb Asian lettuce wraps to girls wearing too many accessories and not enough underwear.

So far, I'd learned that food service really wasn't for me. Handling meals all day leaves a weird stench on your fingertips. It smells like nothing else in the world, and won't wash off either. I'd also learned that the squishiness of the food bothered me too. I found myself dreaming of firm substances, things that wouldn't rot, sour, or jiggle.

Still, I'm glad that I started working there, because the restaurant was where Jarvis found me—and that's where my life changed.

I WAS TURNING A CORNER, balancing a plate of *huevos rancheros* in each hand, when I spotted him in my section, one leg crossed over the other, intently reading a copy of the Chronicle of Higher Education. He looked as relaxed as a grandfather on a porch during a summer rain.

But if there's one thing I remembered about Jarvis, it's that there no such thing as a coincidence when he's around. He was here for a reason—and it was probably me.

I walked up to him hesitantly.

"The eagle flies at morning light," I said.

"With the might of a thousand armies," he replied. His eyes flicked up briefly. He was smiling.

It was the code to the Owl and Pigeons, our secret society at Harvard.

I have two major secrets in my life, and now you know the first one. I went to Harvard University.

I never really talk about it. People really look at you differently. We call it "dropping the H-bomb". Sometimes people think that every person who goes there is loaded with money. That's not even remotely true. Lots of ordinary kids are swimming eyeball-deep in the two hundred thousand dollars in loans that they take out to afford the degree. Those are the middle-class kids. The really poor ones have the best deal. If your parents together earn less than fifty grand a year, Harvard doesn't make you pay a cent.

Jarvis had been one of those poor kids.

He'd told me that he was from Detroit. His father had been a spot welder on the auto assembly lines until he got laid off, and then he didn't work for ten years. Jarvis had told me about his family the first time either of us had ever gotten drunk, in his dorm room on a Friday night. I remember that he'd been so poor in college that he couldn't even afford textbooks. He'd borrow a classmate's books, read the next two weeks of assignments in a single night, scribbling notes.

Sometimes Jarvis would host poker nights for wealthy freshmen. He'd get them drunk, then beat their pants off at the card table. I remember people losing hundreds of dollars to him. Beating Harvard undergraduates at games of strategy isn't any small peanuts either, as you can imagine. Still, everybody knew that he needed the money, so nobody ever begrudged him the winnings.

In short, he was the kind of guy whom everybody knew was going somewhere.

I wasn't very wealthy either. Some of the other Harvard students had smeared our faces in it. The ones you'd think were smart enough to laugh at all that elitist crap are the ones who embraced it the most. Yapping in their ridiculous lockjaw Boston accent, they'd denied us entrance to all the best parties. We weren't invited into any of the secret fraternities.

So Jarvis and I had decided to invent our own secret society. We'd named it the Owl and Pigeons. We had our first meeting in the basement of an off-campus Italian restaurant and drunk dry sherry boosted from the kitchen. We'd posted fake flyers announcing a dress-up day for anybody who wanted into our group. Nobody had really responded. It'd been a fun but pitiful little way of imitating the rich boys.

And so here we were, ten years later, still using our secret code.

I said earlier that I had two secrets. If you're waiting for the second one, you're going to have to wait a while longer. I'm not going to tell you that one yet.

JARVIS LIFTED his face from the publication. Up close, he looked exactly the same as he had in college. He had shiny cheeks, as though he moisturized with canola oil. Every hair was in its place. He wore a smart gray suit with a black tie. He always looked as if he were about to step onstage.

"How's the breakfast burrito?" he said.

"Today, good," I said. "Yesterday, not so good."

"New recipe?"

"New cook."

"It feels like a long time since college," he said. "Doesn't it?"

"I guess," I said.

His eyes traveled over my sauce-splattered smock. I felt embarrassed. Our old friends were becoming scholars, senators, surgeons. I was on my way to becoming assistant weekend manager.

I tipped my chin up and went on the offensive. "So tell me ... how are *you* earning your daily bread these days?"

"Education," he said.

"Really? I'd always thought you'd be a spook."

"A spook?" He looked perplexed. "You mean a spy?"

"Yeah."

Jarvis laughed. "Are you kidding? Spook hours are *terrible*."

"But you always loved surveillance. Remember Heather Brighton's closet?"

"You bet," he said, smiling at the memory. "Sorry, no government work for me. Too many rules and regulations."

Suddenly I felt impatient with this impromptu

encounter with my past. I wanted to get out of it. "What can I get you for lunch?"

"I have a job opportunity for you," he said. "Where can we talk?"

He looked at me intently, gauging my reaction. Then the tiniest crinkle of amusement appeared at the corner of his mouth. Jarvis knew that I couldn't refuse, not *here*, when he'd seen my day job.

"I'm not off my shift until three," I said.

"Then come into the office tomorrow." He handed me his business card. It said *Kenneth Jarvis, M.S.W., Ph.D. Academic Consultant.*

"What exactly is an academic consultant?" I asked.

"I help high school students get into college."

"Don't they have counselors to do that?"

He shrugged. "Most high school counselors don't have enough time. Or resources. Lots of them are getting canned." He spread his arms wide. "I'm here to fill the gap."

I balanced the card in my hand, feeling its heft, toying with the idea. I'd learned long ago that when Jarvis had an idea, it was a good idea to follow him, because it usually worked out.

"I don't know."

"Come in at nine," he said. "You know you want to."

I must've looked hesitant, because he urged me even harder. "Do it for the O and P."

He stuck out his fist. Our old signature goodbye. I couldn't resist. My fist pounded his in the stupid pattern we'd invented—up, down, twice left, twice right, then three fingersnaps. I hate to say it, but it felt good to have been part of that stupid made-up fraternity.

"All right," I said.

He smiled. "You're making the right decision, Jake."

"Speaking of decisions, have you decided what you want?"

"What's good here?"

"I told you the breakfast burrito was okay."

"Can you bring me a menu?"

"Sure."

As I went off in search of a menu, he lifted his coffee mug to his lips and went back to his newspaper. When I returned, the mug and the paper had been laid on the table —but Jarvis was gone.

TWO

Here's a fun fact that I learned recently: There are 600,000 doctors in the United States, but there are 6,400,000 waiters in the United States.

In other words, a person has more than a ten times greater chance of serving food than of going to medical school.

My head is filled with lots of useless knowledge like that. I don't know how it accumulates, but it has, ever since I was a little boy. Names, places, histories, polysyllabic chemical compounds—mental junk.

Not that it ever benefits me. After all, triviahounds are on nobody's preferred list. We don't get upgraded to VIP suites at hotels. No lingerie model flirts with us. The chef never visits our table to see how we liked the meal. At the very best, people give us a curious tilt of the head, a crinkled brow, and a mystified sound like *hm*. At worst, they slash our tires.

Basically, we are trivial.

I know that Jarvis remembered this about me, and maybe that's why he sought me out. I had absolutely no secrets from that guy. He'd seen me at my worst moments. Even Ivy League students act really dumb sometimes.

So there I was now, inching along the slow 'n' go traffic on the freeway toward Jarvis' office. I hate how nobody walks in Los Angeles. You've got the second-largest city in America, over ten million people, over twenty million legs, and yet almost nobody is using any of them unless it's on an elliptical at a gym. Not that I was any different, obviously.

I'd dressed in a clean Oxford blue shirt with pleated khaki slacks. It was a bland look, but I didn't have anything else for a proper job interview. Of course, whether this was even an interview was debatable.

I exited an off-ramp and wound down a long boulevard lined with parking lots, one after another. His office was located in a simple gray office building, well-tended and nicely landscaped with some azaleas and a jacaranda tree exploding in purple blooms.

Inside the lobby, I scanned the occupants' board. There was his office: *Kenneth Jarvis, M.S.W., Ph. D, Suite* 324. That was interesting. Jarvis had earned a doctorate degree, but he hadn't wanted to talk about it. He was the same guy. You had to pry him for information about himself. It was better not to underestimate him.

The elevator was bare and simple, as was the third-floor hallway. Sedate gray paint, cheap wainscoting panels. Unimpressed, I felt my eyelids fogging over.

Jarvis' suite featured an absolutely average door, painted the same gray as the walls. I pressed my ear to it. There was no sound from the space behind. Just silence. All in all, I was beginning to believe that this building felt like a place where nothing important had ever happened.

I rapped my knuckles briskly on the door. There was a sudden scuffle inside, then the metallic chunk of a file drawer slamming shut. Finally I heard the soft brushing sound of shoes crossing carpet.

A very plain woman opened the door, dressed in a plain blue business suit with shoulder pads. I don't know why she was wearing shoulder pads, because she wasn't going to be tackling anybody on a fourth down. Her brown hair was cut into a forgettable bob. She probably drove a minivan.

"Can I help you?" she asked.

"I have an appointment with Jarvis," I said.

"Are you Jake Logan?"

I nodded. "That's me."

She moved aside, holding the door open. "Please come in. I'll let Mr. Jarvis know you're here."

I stepped inside. The windowless suite was nearly as spartan as the hallway. There was a pair of new armchairs with green fabric near the door. A small, low table had been placed between them, on which sat a neat pile of recent magazines. In a far corner huddled a small refrigerator. I stared at it. Something about it reminded me of the refrigerators that had been on the sets of all the film productions I'd worked on. Then I realized that I'd probably just been an actor for too long. I'd forgotten what real life was like.

The secretary quietly assumed her position at her chair. There were only three items on the desk—a telephone, a stapler, and a computer. It was turned off. I thought about my own desk at home with its piles of unopened mail and scraps of paper, and wondered what kind of personality kept such a pristine desk.

The secretary pressed a button on the phone. "Mister Jarvis, Jake is here."

This seemed like an unnecessary formality. The only other door in the office was less than ten feet away. I don't have much patience for any type of indirectness. In fact, I'd studied a little about China's traditionally heavy bureaucracy, and how their historically intricate levels of public officialdom led to the acceptance of central Communist control in the twentieth century. It's all associated with the etymology of the word *mandarin*.

But that's just my embarrassing brain. It's always revving in fifth gear.

Here, though, in Jarvis' office, it was probably safe to be my real self. I watched the secretary begin typing. She was the weirdest typist I've ever seen. Her fingers were jabbing at the keyboard and her shoulders were hunched high as though someone had run an electric current through them. She looked like some kind of queer gangly puppet putting on a show.

But before I could peer over her shoulder to see the document, Jarvis entered the room.

"I knew you'd show up," he said.

"I don't like to disappoint," I said.

He held open the door to his office and gestured for me to enter.

THREE

Jarvis' office was rather sumptuous. There was heavy furniture, immaculate cream carpeting. I sat down on a leather sofa. He sat behind his large oaken desk. It was heavy with presence.

Then I noticed a print of *The School of Athens* hanging on the wall. The one by Raphael.

"That's appropriate," I said.

"At first I had a mirror," he said, "but I noticed that the parents were primping themselves while I was talking."

I stretched my arms over my head. It felt comfortable here. "I'm sorry we fell out of touch," I said. "It was my fault."

"No, it was mine," he replied. "I've had my head down, working like a dog trying to get ahead of the world." He gestured to a picture of himself with a woman and a toddler. "Plus I've got a little baby bird crying for worms."

I inspected the photo. His wife and child looked beautiful and nearly perfect, like one of those studio shots that come inside of new picture frames.

"She's a great partner," he said. "The baby has been a little stressful, but we're okay."

I felt regret that I hadn't tried to contact him. "You know, if I'd only known you were in Los Angeles—"

Jarvis seemed uncomfortable. "There's nothing we can do about that. Besides, I knew you were busy."

"How?"

"The alumni grapevine. They talk about you. Don't you ever go on the Internet?"

"I try not to," I said, and meant it. If you're a public figure, even a D-list actor like me, it's better not to.

"You have a fanbase," he said.

"As far as I know," I said, "my fanbase consists of one guy in Oregon who emails me a picture of his genitals every Saturday night."

"So block his email."

"I have. He keeps changing it."

Jarvis shrugged. "The modern world."

He handed me a can of soda and dropped into one of the heavy leather chairs.

"So do you know what I did after graduation?" he said.

I honestly couldn't recall. "Tell me."

"I stayed at Harvard and worked in admissions."

That didn't surprise me. "I remember you giving campus tours on Sunday mornings while the rest of us were hungover," I said.

He nodded. "And I ended up staying five more years to work. Do you know when I finally knew it was time to leave?"

I sipped my lemon-lime soda and felt the bubbles tickle the inside of my mouth. "When?"

"The day I realized that parents were willing to pay a

lot of money to someone who had worked in Harvard's admissions office."

"And that someone would be you."

"Exactly."

Jarvis sat back and steepled his fingers. His tongue probed the inside of his cheek. It looked like a massive secret trying to explode out the side of his face.

I cleared my throat. "So helicopter parents drag their miserably overachieving children into this office to beg for your Ivy League connections."

"More or less."

"That could give you a God complex."

He smiled. "Believe me, I am very human."

"Can I ask what you charge them?"

He shrugged. "It's flexible, depending on family income. But most of my clients do come from wealthy households."

This conversation was making me realize something. I wasn't really in the grown-up world yet. Not while acting and waiting tables. Jarvis, on the other hand, had learned how life really worked. We were the same age, but I was still a teenager.

"You still haven't explained what you need from me," I said.

Jarvis nodded. "Despite what people may think, I don't have a magic wand. Students who want to be considered by a competitive university must be exceptional individuals."

"So what do you do?"

He waved his hand in a broad gesture. "God, what don't I do? Advise them on curriculum, send them on community service trips, run workshops, browbeat teachers into giving great recommendation letters."

Then he got to his feet and walked around the heavy

desk to his chair. "But I have one student who has requested more personalized help." He eyed me closely.

"What kind of help?" I said.

"She needs someone who can help her get into Harvard."

"I don't understand."

"She needs a tutor."

"Okay."

I must've looked like I still wasn't getting it, because Jarvis became very direct.

"Jake," he said, "I want you to be her tutor."

FOUR

The statement sank between us like a fat aunt into a couch. I waited for him to keep talking.

"I know you're smart enough," Jarvis said. "And a big part of successful tutoring is acting."

"But I'm not qualified to teach," I said. "For many reasons. You know what I'm talking about."

"Maybe, but this isn't teaching. There is no qualifying test to become a tutor. When someone hires you, that's when you become one."

"Isn't there somebody else?"

"Nobody that I can trust. This student is *very* special."

I was a little disappointed. This wasn't the life-changing offer I'd expected. There would be no flights to Paris, no lunches with Arabian oil sheiks. Still, it represented a change, and that was what I needed most.

"What's the pay?" I asked.

"I can offer you twenty dollars an hour. It's low because you have no experience." Then he added reassuringly: "I'm sure it'll go up after your first review."

On a busy night, my job at the Earthen Jug paid me

about the same. And this job wouldn't make me touch anything squishy. I could stay clean. I could sit down. I could use big words without losing any tips.

It sounded like a trade up. But I didn't want to let Jarvis know this yet.

"I don't know," I said. "Tell me more about this very special student."

He nodded. Reaching inside his desk, he removed an inch-thick manila file folder.

"Her name is April Kim. Age seventeen, resident of Bel Air, youngest of two children. She's a senior at Chandler-Beacon—that's the best high school on the West Coast. Very accomplished. She's class treasurer, varsity soccer captain, president of fourteen student clubs, co-winner of the Intel Science Talent Search, fluent in Korean, Spanish, and Farsi. I can keep going, if you want."

I'm not easily impressed, but this floored me. This girl April was playing the game of life at a whole different level. It seemed that the best thing I could do would be to serve her lunch and get out of her way.

Jarvis continued: "You would meet with her every day from three to six o'clock. Her parents work very late and want someone supervising her after-school studies."

"Which includes what?"

"First, you'd prepare her for the SAT. Then you'd help prepare her college applications. Throughout you'll be helping with her homework and projects as she needs. I'm sure other things will crop up. But all of this is directed towards the same purpose."

"Admission to Harvard," I said.

"Exactly. Her parents have engineered her entire life towards this single goal."

"Which is why you want someone who attended

Harvard." I thought of the pressure this girl must feel and rubbed my eyes in pain. "My God, Jarvis. Who *are* these people?"

He tapped his pen against the desk. "Wealthy importers."

"What do they import?"

"It's not really my business to know. I'm guessing clothing, electronics, packaged food, whatever. They're Korean."

"Hm."

"They've also made a killing in California real estate since Korea lifted the cap on investment in foreign residential properties." He seemed to sense my unease. "Listen, Jake, don't think too much about the parents. You probably won't even meet them. They work too much."

He let the words drop. We sat in silence for a moment.

"I'd have to quit waiting tables," I finally said.

"I understand."

"And what if this doesn't work out?"

"It will. April's going to love you. And when you're finished with her, there will be others. We have two hundred students here."

That was a nice incentive. I twiddled with my sock. It was a bad habit. Tutoring this girl wasn't going to be a piece of cake, but Jarvis had correctly guessed that it was my best option right now.

"Okay," I said.

Beaming, Jarvis walked around the desk and clapped me around the shoulders. I stiffened. He never expressed himself like this.

"I knew you would take it," he said. "You're still the same, Jake Logan. Dependable."

"Not really," I said. "I am an actor, after all."

He ignored the comment and returned to his desk. "So

you must know that parents talk a lot. If you do a good job, it could expose us to a whole new segment of the Los Angeles market."

"I have one question. How did you know I would take it?"

"Because you twiddled with your sock. That's your tell."

"So that's how—"

"—I won all that money in poker at college. Yes. Everyone has a tell."

"You bastard."

He laughed as he handed me a heavy plastic shopping bag that had been stapled shut. It was filled with books. "These are your materials," Jarvis said. "Her address is inside too. Good luck."

FIVE

On my way home that afternoon, I came up with two excellent reasons to call Jarvis and tell him that I'd changed my mind.

The first is that I'd become involved in one of the most marginal occupations that has ever existed. Take it from me. We actors are totally scumbags—deceitful, manipulative, narcissistic. We usually aren't too bright either. Thinking just gets in the way, which is probably why I'd never been more than halfway decent at the craft. My brain is always running.

The second reason is the other secret. The one that I don't want to tell you yet.

I emailed my full resume to Jarvis that night and lay awake for a long time thinking about this sudden change of occupation. Tutoring a teenager honestly didn't seem too difficult. No sixteen-year-old, no matter how great an over-achiever, was likely stand up to an adult. I would hold control.

Most importantly, I was an actor. I could slip into character if necessary. If she wanted a chat buddy, I could give her that. If she wanted a hardass slave driver, I could give her that too. No matter what, she would feel the illusion of comfort. It would be an improv class in real time.

Confident, I finally fell asleep with a smile on my face. When I woke up, Jarvis had already emailed me with the information that my first session with April would be that same afternoon. He included the address and reminded me not to be late.

I immediately called in sick to the Earthen Jug. They weren't too happy to hear from me. I pretended to be sick and regretful. I don't know if it worked. If they think I'd really miss a day refilling waters, then they didn't really know me.

Later that morning, I carried the bag of materials up the staircase of my apartment building to the roof. This was my favorite getaway. I kept a folding slingback chair up here, hidden behind an air conditioner.

I looked around. It was an overcast morning. Twelve blocks from the beach meant heavy marine layer. By noon, the gray gloom would burn off and the tarry rooftop would be too hot for bare feet. But right now the place felt balmy and soothing. I fell back into the chair and opened the bag.

Inside I found a galaxy of tutoring materials. There were vocabulary flashcards. A book of SAT practice exercises. A homework planner. A college guide. An interview guide. A book with the delicious title of *50 Successful Harvard Application Essays*.

I closed the bag, tilted my head back, and closed my eyes. I hadn't prepared like this for Harvard. I'd just applied on a whim. My essay had been a tongue-in-cheek first draft about the history of pocket lint. That's no joke. Even though I'd had good high school grades, I was as surprised as anybody when the thick letter from Cambridge arrived.

They must've liked the jazz band. That's one part of my history that's kind of embarrassing. I'd been part of a jazz vocal ensemble in high school. I could always harmonize, and my teacher had said why ruin such a good tenor screaming rock songs. So for the next three years I'd sung Mel Torme tunes at competitions with three other kids.

But the teacher had booted me out right quick the moment my voice dropped. The dismissal had been merciless and cold. I'd been angry at the time, but if I could meet him now, I'd thank him. He prepared me for the world of acting, which is even worse.

I woke up with the sun blazing on my face and blue sky overhead. I didn't even remember falling asleep. It was one thirty. I hurried downstairs to shower and shave, then saw my face in the mirror.

It was sunburned. I looked redder than a crabshell.

Smearing lotion didn't help. I was going to look like a fool. I swore at myself as I got dressed in jeans and a polo shirt. I figured that tutors shouldn't draw attention to themselves by looking either too formal or too scruffy.

With April's address in my hand, I climbed into my car. I'd been meaning to buy a new one for the longest time. Never before has a more rickety contraption been steered through the streets of this city. It was held together with twine, spit, and prayer.

It took three attempts, but soon the engine sputtered to life with all the energy of an aging rock star headed to an eight a.m. therapy session. I looked at the address in my hand, then pointed the wheels towards Bel-Air.

SIX

As I climbed into the residential hills above Sunset Boulevard, my little four-banger engine revved even more loudly, so I slowed down and admired the homes sliding past my windows.

These glassy homes were temples to modernity. They had been built years ago in the mid-twentieth-century style, covered in vast panes of reflective glass. I shuddered when I thought of how much air conditioning those families must use. Then I remembered that rich people didn't have to worry about those things.

I drove along, feeling uncomfortable. Bel Air was unfamiliar territory. The people here had done something right to afford these homes. I started to feel bad about my own life decisions.

Soon the air grew thinner, the tree trunks thicker, the scent of orange blossoms heavier. The traffic on the boulevard below faded to a distant murmur. I kept an eye on the address numbers painted on the curbs. When I saw April's number, I stepped on the brakes and skidded to a halt.

An ivy-covered wall dominated the street, at least

fifteen feet high. It was also totally impenetrable, except for the black wrought-iron gate. Above the callbox there was a small sign with a car icon and a red X.

No parking on property. I parked on the street, facing downhill, turned the tires toward the curb, and set the handbrake. Driving isn't really my cup of tea, probably because I live in Los Angeles. In fact, my life would improve if that damn car *did* roll into a canyon.

I stepped out, took my materials, and went to the callbox. The instructions told me to press the pound sign, so I did. On the first ring, a garbled inhuman voice barked something incomprehensible. Then the gate silently swung inward.

I clutched my bag to my side and peered into the property. Ahead lay a dark and narrow footpath, bordered by two rows of oaks and their low-hanging branches. Heavy undergrowth crowded the way. Those glassy modern homes felt a world away.

I gulped and took my first tentative step. The sunlight that had dappled my arms disappeared, and its warmth too; a chill crept up the skin of my back and raised goosebumps all over my body. I gripped my bag close to my hip as I moved further along the walk. Why couldn't this girl live in a regular house? Or apartment?

As I moved forward, the trees pressed ever closer, and I gritted my teeth. There seemed to be no end to this tunnel. Sweat dripped into the corner of my eyes. Gnats hovered around my cheeks. A part of me wanted to turn back, head down the hill, return to my lowlander comfort. But a stronger part of me needed to see what lay ahead.

At last the trail curved, and I was looking at an elaborate formal garden. I'm no expert on landscaping, but it seemed like someone had desperately tried to recreate a classic

Tudor English estate, with its severe rows of box hedges and knotted arrangements of bushes and flowers. In the center was a sundial, encircled by a ring of brass arrows on the ground.

I whistled softly to myself. On movie sets there'd always been rumors about enormous hidden estates perched up in the Santa Monica Mountains. This was one of them.

The mansion lay behind it, and I followed the pave-stones around the garden to get a better view. Even though the home was right in front of me, it was hard to see. This was partly because it was hidden by thick foliage. Not even the fabled California sunlight could penetrate the shrubbery that cloaked the walls. Only once did I catch a glimpse of charcoal-colored brick beneath the thick green ivy. Even now, after everything that happened, I still couldn't describe the home.

I started up the front walk. I was startled as the wide front door suddenly shuddered in its frame. Then jerked again, more violently. Someone was trying to open it from the inside.

One more jerk, and the heavy slab broke loose of the frame and swung inwards. I squinted into the dark aperture and shifted my weight to my other foot. A small figure finally hobbled out of the darkness.

It was a dwarf.

She was Asian and stood no higher than my waist. Her back was hunched up on the left side, forcing her head down to the right. One leg had been severely crippled. It was bowlegged and turned outwards.

The creature peered around until her gaze landed on me. Then her hugely round left eyeball squinted sharply, and its intense gaze pierced me so hard that my stomach plunged. It felt like being watched by an evil squid.

"Is this April Kim's house?" I said. As though anyone could've accidentally stumbled onto this place.

The dwarf didn't answer. Her evil squint-eye stayed fixed on me. Then she lurched around and shuffled back into the darkness, her misshapen hump heaving. She was an authentically ugly creature, one of the losers of the genetic lottery.

But the door stayed open.

I approached the door and paused. It's not that I was nervous. I just wanted to appreciate the moment. This was one of the weirdest situations in my life—and coming from someone who works in the entertainment industry, that's saying a lot.

I removed my sunglasses and crossed into the dark mansion.

SEVEN

As my eyes adjusted to the darkness, I discovered myself standing in a very high, dark foyer. Its wooden walls were ornately carved with hundreds of small Gothic spires like stalagmites. In the center of the room was a heavy octagonal table.

It was a perfect replica of an English manor—here in the hills of Los Angeles.

I had just taken a step toward the table when a horrible squawking erupted at my back. It was the dwarf. She had one hand on her hip. Her other index finger was jabbing at my feet while a torrent of angry words spat out from between her blubbery lips.

"I don't understand you," I said.

The torrent only grew stronger. Her cheeks were growing redder. And every time I stepped backwards, it doubled in intensity.

She kept gesturing near the door. Then I noticed a pile of boots, slippers, and shoes near the door.

Ah. That was it.

I kicked off my shoes into the pile. "I'm sorry, I didn't know this was Asia."

The dwarf immediately straightened my shoes so that the toes were facing the door. She was mumbling to herself in the way that shut-ins sometimes do. Then she turned, lurched down the hall, and disappeared.

That was my welcome to April's house.

Standing alone, all my senses were on high alert. In a side room, I noticed a small movement and peered more closely.

Another small Asian woman sat cross-legged on the floor. This one wasn't deformed, but she was haunted, as though she'd survived a war. Time and wrinkles had ravaged her face and nearly squinched her eyes shut.

I looked down at her hands. They were scrubbing out a ceramic jar with a sponge. The jar looked clean to me. It seemed thought she just might be comforting herself with the repetitive motion.

Then something was pulling on my sleeve. It was the dwarf. She was gesturing towards another wing of the house.

I followed the dwarf, her freakish hump rising up and down with every step. We entered a dark hallway with several doors on either side. One was open. Inside was a bare white bedroom with a white comforter and a single rack of clothing. It looked like a prisoner's cell.

But I couldn't explore it, because my guide had arrived at the furthest door and pushed it open. A flash of sunlight blinded me as I entered.

I've got a fetish about libraries. That's probably no surprise to you. In fact, whenever I was shooting on location, as soon as the A.D. shouted "wrap", I headed straight for the nearest bookstore, to inspect the offerings. Harvard probably burned that into me.

This room, however, could shame even the grandest of libraries at the Ivy League. It was sunny, airy, and spacious. There were thirty-foot bookshelves with rolling stepladders. I'd never seen anything like it in a private home.

In the center of the room was a massive cherrywood desk. And sitting behind that desk was a teenage girl.

It was April Kim.

EIGHT

She was petite, no more than five feet tall, with thin arms and high cheekbones. She wore a business suit. Her eyeliner had been perfectly applied. Her makeup was conference-room ready. A headset was perched on her coiffed hairdo.

I stood near the doorway, hands folded, and waited for her conversation to end.

"Listen," the teenager was saying, "here's the bottom line. Caroline may be captain of the varsity field hockey, but she wasn't picked for her intelligence. She's a figurehead and she knows it. I am the real student liaison with the athletic department, and I say that we are keeping the pet store sponsorship. My soccer squad needs their end-of-year support for the nationals in Maryland."

I shifted in my sock feet, hoping to get her attention. It didn't work.

"I'm *sorry* that she's upset. Listen, if Caroline wants to set up a fundraiser to replace that lost revenue, then I'll be happy to take a meeting. Good. Let's touch base on Thursday between third and fourth mods. Talk soon."

She ripped off the headset, then reached into her desk drawer. I craned my head. It was packed with pills.

"I'm starting to think life is too short for this much stress," she said out loud. She swallowed a couple of pills with a sip of water.

Then April stared out one of the narrow vertical windows towards the formal gardens beyond. The expression on her face was wistful.

I cleared my throat, and April finally turned her head. Her gaze was like a pair of hot searchlights sweeping across me. "And who are you?"

"Jake Logan," I said, "your tutor. Kenneth Jarvis sent me."

"Of course," she replied.

I crossed the room and stuck out my hand. She looked at it like it had been hacked off a plague victim, but shook it anyways. She had a limp handshake. It was how I imagined a princess would shake.

I stepped back. She looked me up and down from head to toe. "Tutors. You always seem so *shabby*."

"You've had tutors before?"

She waved her hand in the air. "Only for English, history, art, science, music, math, reading, grammar, philosophy, public speaking, debate, and posture. So yes. You people are like clouds. You come and go."

I took a seat in the low club chair next to her desk. She swiveled to face me. I could see that the business suit was most likely a Donna Karan. On her feet were a pair of black heels. I was finding it hard to believe that she was sixteen years old.

"So what did Jarvis tell you?" she said.

"About what?"

"About me."

"He said that you want to get into Harvard."

"I don't *want* to get into Harvard. I *will* get into Harvard."

"That's the spirit."

She sighed. "My last SAT tutor was condescending too."

"Did you like him?"

"Do you see him here?"

I shifted in my seat. It wouldn't be good to argue during the first session. "Why don't you tell me a little about yourself?"

She sighed again and ticked off the major points on her fingers. "Born in Korea, grew up in this prison. Dad works hundred-hour weeks and goes to China for business a lot. Raised by dwarf nanny. The end."

Her eyes fixed on mine, daring me to challenge this abridged version of herself.

"But that leaves out all the interesting parts," I said.

"That's all that matters."

"No," I said, "that's just you on paper. Nixon looked good on paper too. He turned out to be a racist, paranoid mad bomber."

Too late I realized that this was a terrible comparison to be making, but fortunately she shrugged it off. My words were unimportant to her. She'd probably dealt with lots of guys just like me.

I suddenly stood up and crossed the room to inspect some kendo equipment stacked in a corner. There was a stick and face mask.

"That's mine," she noted.

I ignored her. "What do you think of Jarvis?"

"He's not demanding enough."

I raised my eyebrows. "Really? He's known as a taskmaster."

"Not to me."

"He did say you were very special."

"In the drooling way, no. In the hard-to-please way, yes." She was holding my gaze again. I got the feeling that I was being put through my paces. Poked and prodded.

Her tongue snaked out to the corner of her mouth, and signs of a hidden agenda emerged in her shifty eyes. "What university did you graduate from, Jake?"

There was no reason to drop the H-bomb yet, so I demurred. "I can't say."

"Oh God. You went to Cal State or something."

"No."

"Brigham Young?"

"No, I like coffee too much."

"The Citadel?"

"I can't say because it's against company policy." Then I laid it on a little thicker. "Plus other parents might get jealous."

April seemed to accept that. Then she straightened her shoulders and a look of smug entitlement spread across her face. "I'm only handing over my future to the very best."

"And Jarvis only hires the very best. You can trust his judgment."

She paused, as though making up her mind. Then her phone vibrated.

April looked at the display and scowled. She put the headset back on and picked up the call. "Jenna. We have a group project on Othello due on Tuesday and you haven't yet checked out the book that Mr. Mangrove assigned you."

I was morbidly fascinated in this conversation and listened in.

"No," she continued, "you did *not* drive all the way to Santa Monica Library for it. I know because I checked out that copy last week. Please stop crying. I'm just trying to cover myself too. Look, unless you start pulling your weight, I'm going to be forced to lobby Mister Mangrove to have you reassigned to a different group project. I'm sorry. Let's touch base tomorrow between seventh and eighth mods." She ended the call and stenciled something into the touchpad.

"That's tough love," I said.

"If you want something done right," she replied, "you've got to do it yourself."

"It's always been my motto," I lied. "So what should we do today?"

"Not much." April began stuffing several books of musical notation into a fancy shoulder bag. "I've got choir practice in twenty minutes and can't be late. The director is *such* a type A personality, it's ridiculous."

"That's too bad."

She crossed the room and stabbed my chest with an index finger. "But we're on for three o'clock tomorrow. I'll stay longer, I promise. Mina will let you out. And FYI, don't mess with her. She's got a chip on her shoulder the size of Gibraltar."

April breezed past me and out the door, as though she were late for a conference call with investors in Hong Kong. The masculine smell of purpose and resolve lingered in the air after she left.

I sat in the chair, stunned, my arms hanging loosely down to the floor.

The hunchbacked dwarf, Mina, entered the room and barked something at me. From her gestures it was pretty clear what she meant.

Dazed, I walked like a zombie back down the hallway to the foyer, the dwarf was practically nipping at my heels. I slipped on my shoes and stepped outside. The front door slammed behind me.

Outside, with birds singing, the sun shining, I stood on the front stoop wondering what the hell I had just signed up for.

NINE

That night, looking through the materials, I discovered how tough a test the SAT really was.

Students had to know coordinate geometry, unclear antecedents, and words like *catharsis*. They also had to read passages about scintillating topics ranging from Joan of Arc to garden slugs.

I finished an entire practice test, scored it, then figured out how to explain the hardest questions. I would not be caught with my mental pants down again by this little Napoleon.

The next day I called in sick to the Earthen Jug again. I told them that I had malaria. I don't know why I chose that disease. It didn't matter, because nobody there would care enough to check up the possibility of my having contracted such a malady. Soon they'd find somebody else to cover my shifts. That was restaurant work—easy come, easy go.

Then I stood staring at my closet. Tutoring April would require a powerful wardrobe, something that radiated authority. In the back of my closet hung a pinstriped British suit. It was gray and square and had been part of my wardrobe during a role on a mid-season replacement program that had lasted only three episodes. The costume designer had let me keep it. When I opened the jacket at home, I'd found his phone number, along with an obscene note, pinned to the inside lining.

Sweating in the wool, I returned to the mansion in the sky that afternoon. I rang the buzzer at the gate again, was admitted, strode down the long dirt path, rounded the sundial, and rang the front doorbell.

Mina the dwarf cracked the door open. She stared at me with that single squid eye but didn't open the door any further, so I pushed—hard. She stumbled backwards, and soon I was kicking off my shoes.

When I entered April's room, she was flopped upside down on her couch with her phone pressed to her ear. She was wearing Capri pants and a pink t-shirt. Her hair was held up by a cheap hairclip.

"Good afternoon," I said.

She was engrossed in her phone in that special way that teenage girls have, as though they have disappeared bodily into the electron stream.

I listened to her conversation again.

"Wait wait wait!" she was saying, "Was it a real LV? Or was it from Santee Alley? Seriously, if you have a knockoff, we are not speaking again."

I coughed. Her eyes rolled around, spotted me, then rolled back. I was less than spit.

"Hello," I said.

She sighed. "Jess, I have to go. It's my tutor. I know, it sucks. He wants me to work or something." She listens. "Jeff did *not*? Tell me! Right now, you *have* to tell me—"

I dropped my bag and took a seat in the club chair. "April, it's time to start our session."

"I have to go," she said, "call me later." She closed the phone and crossed the floor petulantly.

April plopped herself down behind her desk, but the gargantuan tabletop now seemed to dwarf her. She seemed much more her own age. My elaborate outfit now felt like overkill.

I produced a short stack of photocopies from my bag. "The first piece of business we need to talk about," I said, "is the SAT. Your goal is a perfect score, which only two hundred students earn each test date. So here's a little practice test. I thought we could move through it, section by section—"

She gave a faint shrug and yawned.

"Is there a problem?"

"No."

"Good. Then let's talk strategy. What's the best way to do a sentence completion?" My mouth was making the right noises, but April lolled around in her chair, her limbs splayed out like those of a rag doll.

"April," I said.

"*What*?" Her voice sounded exasperated.

"I need your attention."

"But I've already *done* this a hundred times. I've been doing these since *seventh grade*."

"So you're an expert. Okay. Pretend that I'm an amateur and show me how it's done."

Her eyes found an eraser. It was shaped like an elephant. She picked it up and began inspecting it more closely. I'd lost her again.

"Put down the eraser," I said. "Look at me."

Then her phone buzzed. April grabbed and answered it before the first ring had even ended. As another story poured into her ear, she grew more lively. Her eyes blazed with girlish passion. "Oh my *God*. Was Amelia there? She wasn't supposed to be!"

Sometimes I do things without thinking. I don't regret those moments, but other people sometimes are amazed at their audacity. This was one of those moments.

I reached over, snatched the mobile phone from her hand, dropped it into my bag, and zipped the bag shut.

She looked stunned. Then her mouth came alive. "That was Lisa Rubin, you idiot! Her father owns like half of Long Beach!"

"This is my time," I said, "not yours."

"Give it back."

"Show me how you do a sentence completion."

From inside my bag came the small buzzing. Lisa was calling back. April stamped her feet. A furious little growl built up in her throat and erupted into a scream. She stomped over to a leather couch and dealt it a flurry of small punches. Then she threw herself facedown onto its cushions.

This was a full-blown tantrum.

I lowered my head into my hands. I wasn't tutoring. I was going into a tiger's cage with a whip and a stool.

I stood up and approached April. She had pulled herself up to sitting position, but her lips were pursed tightly and her jaw was thrust forward. She was staring rigidly ahead, as though she were playing robot.

I sat down next to her on the couch. Not too close, but not too far. We both faced straight ahead. I crossed my arms like hers. I matched my breathing to hers. This was mirroring. It felt like the right thing to do.

She shifted her weight uncomfortably and glanced sideways at me. I waited for her to speak but she didn't. Desperate, I spotted a small plush toy on the floor near my feet. It was a monkey. I picked it up.

"Don't touch Monkey," she said.

"Sorry." I handed her the monkey. It sat on her lap.

Then another one of those audacious moments came over me. "Monkey," I said, "does April want to work with Jake today?"

On her lap, the monkey shook its head no. April was playing along.

I tried again. "Monkey, I want you to tell April that Jake understands that she's in a bad mood."

Monkey nodded.

"Then I want you to tell her that Jake's going to come back tomorrow when she's feeling better."

Monkey nodded again. I slapped my hands on my thighs to signal my departure. "Have a good night, Monkey."

I dropped April's phone on the desk and left the room. I didn't look back.

TEN

The next day was sunny, which made me angry.

I hate sunny days, mostly because variety is the spice of life, and by September there've usually been ninety-five continuous days of future melanoma beating down on Los Angeles already. By that time of the year I'd saw off my left foot to get a decent thundershower.

My favorite place to drink is a bar in Hollywood called the Tiki Ti. It's about ten square feet and they've got their priorities straight. No beer, no wine, no food, no soda, no water. Just pure hard liquor and fruit juice.

I didn't care that I had to work that afternoon. April had plunged me into a don't-give-a-damn mood. Sometimes a fruity cocktail, or seven, is exactly what you need to smooth the rough edges. Today, I'd smoothed so many rough edges that I was no longer a man. I was a circle.

That's why, by the time I sauntered onto the Kim grounds, it was almost an hour past our meeting time and my tongue was caked dry. It felt like a huge piece of cotton sitting there in my mouth. I respect people, but only when they respect me back, and April had already forfeited that.

Mina allowed me inside and stared openly from behind her squid eye. I shuffled down the hall and brushed against a pedestal. The rare ebony vase on top spun precariously but stayed up.

I pushed into April's room without a greeting. I fell down into the seat next to her, propped my bare feet on her desk, and spit into a garbage can. It was a real bottom-of-your-throat lugey, one of those that can only be summoned after drinking very thick liquor.

April stared at me, her eyes traveled up and down my beachwear of cargo shorts, t-shirt, and sunglasses.

"You look different," she said.

"Try another euphemism."

"Are you drunk or something? What have you been doing?"

"I can't talk about it."

"Why?"

"You're too young."

"I'm sixteen."

I made a show of taking out my phone. It wasn't a nice one like hers, but I didn't care. I was in that kind of mood. A high-wire act that would be end in either brilliant success or never-ending disaster.

I pretended to dial a number. April said, "You can't call anyone."

"Why not?"

"You're supposed to be paying attention to me."

I snorted. "And you're supposed to be respectful and cooperative, but that hasn't happened yet either, has it?"

Then, with silence in my ear, I pretended that a friend had picked up the other end of the line. "Hey, it's me. What happened to Jonesy after I left? No shit."

I glanced at April. She was watching me with a mixture of fury and fascination. I kept talking.

"Two grand? I've only got, like, a hundred on me. Why'd the judge set the bail so high? That's *bullshit*. I know the guy, and he's *not* a flight risk. Wait, don't bounce yet, I'll go with you. Wait for me. I don't know, maybe twenty minutes."

I ended the call and went for my bag, but April had hooked her foot through the loop. "You can't go," she said.

"We'll make it up another time."

"I *forbid* you from leaving!"

I crooked my head. "What makes you think you have *any* power in this relationship?"

She chewed over that one for a while. She must've realized that she didn't really have an answer, because she opted for the old standby—an *ad hominem* attack.

"You're pathetic," she said, "and you're a terrible liar."

"You," I said, "have got a body full of nerve but not a brain cell in your head. In fact, I clocked you the minute I set foot in this house."

"Is that so?"

"Yep."

"Then tell me about myself," she said. "Who am I?"

"A petty tyrant."

"Proudly."

"A maniac."

"We succeed."

Those were BB pellets, so I swung the cannon towards her. "And a daddy's girl."

That got her. April blinked several times. I saw a big wet glossy tear forming in the corner of her eye. I pushed harder.

"Your parents made you," I said. "Without them, you wouldn't even pass a bowling class at community college."

Her chin was trembling now. "How could you say that?"

She was starting to cry now, so I let the waterworks run.

"You are so *mean*," she said.

"I'm sorry your feelings are hurt," I replied. That, of course, was a lie. Her feelings weren't worth two drips of runny crap to me.

Her fist pounded the desk. "My parents do *not* control me. How could they? I don't even *see* them! I barely *know* them."

"Ask yourself why you work so hard."

"Because that's just what I do."

"No, it's because that's what your *parents* want you to do."

She didn't say anything to that. But her face looked like someone had just slipped a rotten oyster into her morning cereal.

"April," I continued, "I've known families like yours before. You get a B, and they don't love you anymore. Am I right?"

Okay, I allow that I might've crossed a line there. In fact, I'm sure I did, because in a flash there was a whirl of hair and tiny fists beating on me.

I don't remember how I left her house, but I arrived home sure that I had successfully sabotaged my own job. April Kim would have to seek enlightenment from a different tutor.

And the Earthen Jug was suddenly looking pretty good again.

ELEVEN

I knew the voicemail would be waiting for me when I got home from surfing. The only surprise was that it took as long as it did.

Surfing is the only reason to pay the astronomical rent needed to live near a beach. Under my arm was slung a nine-foot longboard. It's considered a beginner's board, which causes other guys in the lineup to sometimes harass me. I don't care if they make fun of me. Anybody who surfs in Los Angeles is a dilettante anyways, because the best waves are closer to San Diego, and everybody knows it.

That's me—unemployed actor, surfer, former waiter. Unless you live in California, you must think I'm an absolute joke, and I wouldn't blame you. Sometimes I wonder myself too.

The voicemail was from Jarvis. He'd gotten a disturbing phone call from April. He needed to talk with me, in person, first thing in the morning. He must've forgotten that first thing in the morning for me is always a bowl of corn flakes and some stretching.

But the next day I went knocking on the unassuming

gray door of his office anyways. That mopey secretary opened it as though she'd never touched a door before. Her desk was still spic-n-span, as was her freakshow typing style. I edged in toward the screen, trying to glimpse the document, but Jarvis popped out of his office at that precise moment, so I backed off.

Once we were inside his private office, he closed the door gently. "So tell me what happened?"

I shrugged and lay down on his couch with my hands crossed behind my head. We'd been roommates for a summer, and it felt natural to kick back, like a dorm-room study session. "You tell me what she said first."

"No, I want to know your story." He opened his palms. "Jake, I'm on your side. You know that."

"The short story," I said, "is that she's *insane.*"

"Well, she's a teenager. The hormones, the stress—"

I interrupted. "No, this is more than that. I'm saying this girl has fourteen different personalities."

"But—"

I cut him off. "Listen to me. When I walk into that house, I don't know whether I'm going to be facing Donald Trump, Blanche Dubois, or Jim Henson."

He nodded, seeming to understand. "No one in her family is low maintenance."

"I sense that."

We sat there, not saying anything for a moment.

"Do you think there's anything you could do differently?" he said.

I held my hands up in a gesture of surrender. "I've played all the angles. I've been the good guy, the bad guy, the don't-give-a-shit guy. My bag of tricks is empty."

I must've looked like my nerves needed steadying, because he stood up and opened a small cabinet. Inside was a classic highboy. He uncorked a decanter filled with rich brown liquid and poured some into two highball glasses. "If it makes you feel any better," he said, "you've outlasted the others."

"How many have there been?"

"Seven." He handed me the glass.

I took the drink and swallowed a big belt of the stuff. It was scotch, and my throat ached at the touch of its sweet roughness. I really love scotch, even though people make fun of me for it, because it's supposed to be a crusty old man's drink. But I don't care. If you spend your life worrying about what other people think of you, then you're bound to be disappointed.

The drink was good. In less than a minute my head felt lighter than a helium balloon. Jarvis was just sitting there, sipping his own drink and watching me as though I were a panda bear on display in a zoo. You could see his mind was off somewhere a million miles away.

Then I felt a little weird about drinking this early—it wasn't even noon—and set my glass down.

"I thought you were a beer kind of guy," I said.

"Yeah, I still am. I keep this stuff mostly to impress rich people."

I reached forward and tasted the liquid again, swishing it around my mouth.

"So April has had *seven* tutors," I said.

"Yes."

"Did they all quit?"

"No, they were fired."

"By you?"

He shook his head. "By April."

That left an obvious question, and it shot out of my

mouth before I could stop it. "Did she fire me? Is that why you're getting me liquored up? To break the bad news?"

He swallowed some scotch and looked at the corner of the room. "No."

"Really?"

"Really."

I propped myself up on the couch. "So I'm going to keep working with her?"

He shrugged. "It's up to you. She really enjoyed spending time with you."

"Shut *up*."

"No, that's what she said this morning. She probably just doesn't know how to show it."

I found that hard to believe. Jarvis looked nervous. His foot was tapping restlessly on the floor, though his hands were steady on his highball glass. He had good solid hands, but you wouldn't ever notice it. There was a lot about him people didn't notice. He kept everything about himself very discreet—except that tapping.

"Would you want to give it another try?" he asked. "I've got assurances from both April and her parents that she'll be much more cooperative this time."

I laughed. "You must be scraping the bottom of the barrel, if you're begging *me* to stay on. Has she really exhausted your entire roster?"

He shrugged again. It was his favorite expression, since it could be taken many ways. "There aren't many people who can handle a girl like April."

"Well, it'd be much easier if I could beat her," I said. I thought this was just a joke, but Jarvis answered it straight.

"You *can* beat her," he said.

"What?"

"In Korea, corporal punishment is very common. She's probably expecting it."

"That," I said, "makes me very happy."

A smile spread across his face. "Before you go, I have something for you to give her." He reached under his desk and produced a rather large gift box wrapped in gold-trimmed foil. "Just tell her it's a little something from me in appreciation of her patience."

I weighed it in my hands. It felt heavy. "You'll do anything to keep this client, won't you?"

"That's what she's accustomed to."

I left the office and went out to my car with the box under my arm. I was curious about it too.

TWELVE

I hadn't planned on getting into a fistfight with April. But it's funny how plans change.

We were standing in her gorgeous study, the leather-bound books stretching up above upon our heads.

Before us, in a pile of shredded wrapping paper, stood a small statue of a horse. It was made of terra cotta.

"What the hell?" I said.

"I'm guessing a Chinese Xian warrior horse," April said.

"How do you know that?"

"The armor over the neck. The blocky style. I learned about them in art history freshman year."

She cleaned away the packing with a sweep of her arm. "Jarvis gives us so many presents like that. We've got them all over the house." She pointed to the hallway. "There's a Mongol warrior out in the hallway. In the kitchen we've got a Japanese woodblock print."

"Why do you think he does that?"

"Probably because my dad talked to him about it. My dad loves collecting Asian art. He keeps most of it in storage."

"Plus, your family is very important to Jarvis."

"Of course," she said. "We pay him a shitload of money."

I had entered the house without a peep and stolen quietly into her study and presented her with the gift. We hadn't said a word about our last session. Now the awkwardness hung around us like a thick fog.

"So I'd like to get to some vocabulary," I asked.

"I guess."

"Try to contain your excitement."

"It's just that I've got a violin recital tonight." She plopped into the chair. I pulled out a set of vocabulary cards that Jarvis had given me.

"What does *sardonic* mean?" I said.

"Sarcastic."

"Good. *Primordial?*"

"Primitive."

"*Recondite?*"

"Hard to understand."

Clearly April had skills, so I ratcheted up the challenge.

"*Surreptitious?*" I said.

"Secret."

"*Captious?*"

"Fault-finding."

"*Cupidity?*"

"Greed." She yawned and sprawled across the chair. "I did that book two summers ago."

I closed the book. "Then you have a good memory."

She lazily twirled a hank of hair. "It's photographic."

Slightly panicked and feeling outclassed, I reached into my bag. "Let's play something different. Something that will ... *boggle* your imagination."

In my hand was Boggle, the word game. It was another emergency item that Jarvis had loaned me.

She made an ugly face. "You *like* that game?"

"It's the favorite pastime of liberal arts majors everywhere."

"I don't want to major in the liberal arts. I want to make money."

"Just try it."

"No way. I played that at piano camp when I was seven. It was too easy even back then."

"Not with my rules," I said. "You have to make a *ten*-letter word to win."

A smug look drew across her face. "Ten letters."

"Yes."

"I'm *so* going to dust you."

"Nobody ever has."

It was a lie, but she wasn't listening. She'd already shaken the cube and set it down. We both peered into the sixteen-letter grid.

Suddenly April smacked the table. "*Eleemosynary*," she said.

My brow wrinkled. "It has to be a real word."

"That *is* a real word."

"Then prove it."

"It means generous."

"Find me a dictionary."

She threw me a small abridged one and I consulted it. I knew that a showpony like that wouldn't be found in a softcover.

"It's not in here," I said.

She sprang to her feet and retrieved an enormous cloth-bound volume from her floor-to-ceiling bookshelves. She teetered across the room and dropped it like a bag of topsoil onto the table, then handed me a magnifying glass. "Check it."

The cover read Oxford English Dictionary. Eyeing her, I flipped the massive cover open. The entries had been printed in tiny 3-point type. I lifted the glass to my eye and found the word.

"*Eleemosynary*. Charitable." I looked up at her. "That is an obnoxious word."

"Then I'm surprised you didn't know it."

I slammed the book shut. "You know, I'm tired of vocabulary games. Let's talk about college instead."

April crossed her arms and legs. She had a bunker mentality right now. "Go ahead," she said.

"It's very difficult to get into Harvard."

April rolled her eyes. She was merely tolerating me, and it pissed me off. I sharpened my toughest knife and prepared for the plunge.

"Tell me," I asked, "what do you think is going to differentiate you from the thousands of other overachieving Asian students who are applying to Harvard?"

April didn't miss a beat. She reached into her desk and slid a document across the desk. "This," she said.

"What is this?" I said.

"My resume," she said.

I cleared my throat and began reading it out loud. "April Kim. President, National Honor Society. President, Spanish Club. President, French Club. Senior class president. Varsity soccer co-captain. Four point eight GPA." By the end of the page, I'd just read the biography of a gifted but by no means unusual student.

In fact, most people would think this kind of success is enough, but it's not. At least not in the way that Harvard defines success. That school doesn't accept well-rounded people anymore. In fact, my class was a mixture of some of the most bizarre, angular talents in the world. One girl had been America's top under-sixteen speed-walking champion. Another guy had made twenty thousand dollars, at age thirteen, in a massively multiplayer online role-playing game. He'd farmed out virtual weapons to a dealer in Beijing, who was later imprisoned by the Chinese government for the offense. And there was the usual assortment of musical and math prodigies.

"This resume is typical," I said. "What makes you *unique*?"

"Keep reading."

I looked down at the edge of the document. I hadn't noticed that there were four more pages.

As I glanced through the rest of April's life, I tried to hide my surprise. She'd been a winner of the Intel Science Talent Search. She'd traveled to Kenya to teach natives how to purify sources of drinking water. She'd debuted at Carnegie Hall at age twelve, playing oboe.

This changed my mind. Of anybody, this girl had a real fighting chance to get accepted by Harvard. But I sure as hell wasn't going to let her know that.

"Well?" she said.

I crumpled up the paper and delivered the next line with my bitchiest attitude.

"I've seen better," I said.

THIRTEEN

A bolt of anger flashed across her eyes, and she leaned forward across the table. "Nobody is better than *me*," she said.

"Just live a little longer," I replied. "There's always somebody smarter, somebody faster, somebody prettier."

Now her entire body was quivering with fury and her tiny fists were clenched. "What makes you think you can come here and dismiss me? You don't even *know* me!"

"Well, you *are* gifted, but—"

"And who are *you?*" she spat. "Some loser who hangs out with teenagers because he can't find a *real* job?"

It was meant to be insulting, but she was giving me too much credit.

Then she was on her feet, her arm was a blur, and suddenly a book was flying towards me like a Chinese star. I rolled onto the floor and it sailed over my head. Then I leapt back to my feet. I'd really done it this time. April had become completely unhinged.

"Okay, it's time to settle down—"

"No," she cried, "I don't *need* to settle down! I *hate* it when people tell me to settle down! It makes me *angrier!*"

Given her personality, I figured that she probably heard that a lot. Then I remembered Jarvis' piece of advice.

"April," I said, "if you don't settle down, you're not going to like what I do next."

"What? Are you going to hit me?" She planted two sassy hands on her flat hips.

"Look—"

"I dare you! Hit me! *Hit me!!*" She was screaming like the damned, mere inches from my face.

I've never struck anybody in my life, but life is a process of change. My hand swiftly smacked her across the cheek.

It surprised both of us. Her fingers searched her cheek, feeling the red shape where the blood was rising. "You *hit* me!"

"I did."

She was speechless. I rushed in, trying to make it better.

"Jarvis said that it was okay in Korea," I said.

"We're not in Korea!"

Rage filled April's eyes. This strategy had clearly not worked.

I watched her cross the study towards her kendo equipment. She picked up her stick and assumed the first position.

"Put that down," I said. "I'm not fighting you."

"I bet you don't even know kendo."

"I do."

She donned her mask and began to advance. Sighing, I took the other kendo stick and reluctantly assumed a defensive position.

"This is no way to resolve our problem," I said.

"I don't *care.*"

I barely know how to use a kendo stick. I had three days of lessons for a brief role on a pulsing embarrassment of a cable program. But I know enough to recognize that April's form was perfect. She showed absolute unity of foot, arm, and voice.

No sooner had I grabbed the other stick than she made the first strike. Her stick cracked across mine with surprising force, but I held it off. Then the butt-end of her stick suddenly stabbed toward my chest, and I deflected that too.

This wasn't any friendly sparring match. She really wanted to hurt me.

It became even more obvious as our battle spilled into the dark hallway. Our sticks clashed, rattling the framed art on the walls. April was a ridiculously aggressive fighter. Soon I found myself on the defensive, edging further and further backwards.

Eventually she pushed me into the foyer, where she raised her stick and brought it down hard. I blocked it even harder, throwing my weight into the move. Our voices yelled out—

—and her stick splintered.

She stood there, staring in shock. Now was the time for my trick move. I only know one, and it's not even from kendo, but it works every time.

I crouched on my left foot, then quickly swung my right heel in a wide circle and swiped the back of her knees. With a small yelp, April buckled and fell backwards onto the carpet. I leapt onto her tiny body, pinned down her arms with my knees, ripped off her mask, and pressed the tip of my stick to the base of her throat.

"Surprised?" I said.

"You do know kendo," she said, breathing hard.

"Yes. And now *you* know res*pect*," I said. "Say it."

She didn't reply. Her eyes flicked over my shoulder instead. I twisted around—just as the guttural roar reached my ears.

It was Mina.

The humpbacked servant was almost on me. She was fishing out a small canister from her pocket. A half-second later, there was a stinging mist in my eyes—and it wasn't potpourri.

It was pepper spray.

I screamed like the damned and fell over onto the carpet. My hands clamped over my face. It felt like someone was grinding my eyeballs through a cheese grater. There was white noise all around my head. Through the staticky fog, I could hear Mina and April yelling.

Then I passed out.

When I woke up, I found myself on the front stoop of the mansion. The front door had been shut firmly. I'd been flung out like yesterday's milk bottles. My arms were thrown carelessly over my head. I must've landed that way.

Then I heard a small clunk nearby. I sat up uneasily on one hand, rubbing my head.

In the garden nearby, April's wizened grandmother was hunched over a hole in the ground. A row of ceramic bowls waited nearby. She was lowering the pots into the ground, one by one.

I inhaled deeply. Even through the ceramic, I noticed a familiar spicy, fermented smell. It was powerful enough to cut through the pain in my head.

It was kimchi.

The smell made me gag. I leaned over and puked into a flower bed. When I was done, I wiped my mouth and looked back.

This made sense. It was autumn. April's grandmother

had probably been raised in total poverty, and so she was still burying kimchi in the back garden during the winter months. It didn't matter that her family were now hugely wealthy, living in the United States. She'd been burying kimchi for years, and she saw no reason to stop now.

I rose to my feet and staggered out of the garden and back through the long tunnel of trees towards my car.

My time with April had finally come to an end. There was no returning after this.

FOURTEEN

The next day, with reddened eyes, I opened the door of Jarvis' office, unannounced. I didn't need an appointment to tell him my plan.

His freakish secretary quickly snapped off her monitor and leaped to her feet. She was hiding something, but I would never figure it out, since this was my last day working as a private tutor.

She looked at me as though I were a reanimated corpse. It would've been preferable. I felt hideous. My face had broken out in rashes and bumps from the spray.

"I'm going to talk to Jarvis," I said, without breaking stride.

"Please, you can't go in there—"

Ignoring her, I pushed into his office. Jarvis quickly dropped something into the drawer of his desk and slammed it shut. "Jake! I didn't know—"

"I quit."

He harrumphed and shook his head. It dawned on me that he was beginning to regard me as a lightweight. "Is she really that bad?" he said.

"I think quitting is a very reasonable response to getting pepper sprayed by my student's maid."

He tilted his head, and I realized he was staring at my face. "Mina did that to you? What did you do to her?"

"Nothing."

"There must've been some reason."

"April and I were fighting."

His eyes grew wise. "Hand to hand?"

"Kendo. You said corporal punishment was okay."

Jarvis looked suddenly annoyed. "Yeah, Jake, maybe a rap on the knuckles. Not armored combat."

"We weren't armored. It was more like ... a spontaneous eruption of hostility. Look, it doesn't matter. I can't work with her anymore."

He removed his glasses and rubbed his nose. "Why?"

"I don't trust her."

"Really."

"Yes. I don't trust anything she says or does."

"Nothing?"

"Nothing. She's a human-shaped bag of lies."

"Do you think she trusts you?"

I shrugged. The thought hadn't occurred to me.

He perched himself on the arm of his chair. "At risk of sounding totally unprofessional, Jake, let me give you some advice."

"Okay."

He cleared his throat. "Tutoring is like dating. They're both about building solid relationships. That requires building trust. And building trust takes time. I'll give you a couple days to think about your resignation."

"I don't need it."

"I'll give it to you anyways."

"Whatever," I said.

He pressed me. "I'll call you tomorrow."

"There's no cell reception at the beach. You'll have to visit personally."

"Don't tempt me."

I wheeled around to leave—and promptly walked into the doorframe.

"That's my trick door," he said. "It slides around to keep people from doing unwise things."

I managed to get out the second time. His mopey secretary managed a sickly smile as she held open the outer door. It was the nicest thing she'd ever done for me.

FIFTEEN

I stared at my phone. It had a matte finish, was cobalt blue, and had been placed on its charger, which sat on a small end table next to my sad couch. This was the nicest thing that I owned. It has to be, for an actor. We live and die by the phone—that last-minute audition, that anxiously awaited callback.

I wasn't waiting for Jarvis to call. My tutoring days with April Kim were finished. They'd been rolled in a carpet, duct-taped, and dropped off a bridge.

I was waiting for my agent to call.

Everybody I know agrees that there are two types of agents. One type is flattering, expert in the art of body language, brilliant at telling you exactly what you want to hear. The other type is so obviously reptilian that you could make shoes out of his skin.

My agent was the second type. The only reason I stayed with his unctuous, smarmy, lying mug was that he'd gotten me work in the past. I was hanging onto hope that he might do it again in the future.

I'd left a message earlier in the morning with his

assistant. She was a sad-faced girl, fresh out of college, who walked unsteadily in heels like a baby giraffe. She dreamed of becoming a producer in a way that made you feel sorry for her. She was also a good girl, which meant she wouldn't last long in his office.

Now it was three hours later, and I hadn't heard back yet. I knew deep in my heart of hearts that agonizing was useless. Even during the best of times, Lew waited several days to return my calls.

That was then.

Today, the contest shows have killed much of the acting business. I don't call them reality shows, because there's nothing real about spending a month on a remote island for a million dollars. Their effect on actors has been severe. The bullseye has pulled so far away. It's nearly impossible to get a part in a drama or sitcom. I can't even get a part in my hair.

So I spent an hour ambling down Venice Beach with my hands in my pockets. That's something that every person should do at least once in life. Venice is a total sideshow. I remember one time a guy tried to sell me a piece of magic string. Drifters, misfits, grinders with hopes of starting over —all eventually find themselves here, staring out at the blue limit of their dreams.

Eventually, even the rhythms of the drum circle disappeared behind the setting sun. I ducked into a dirty Thai restaurant for dinner and swallowed the food without tasting it. Living for myself felt great when things were high, but it was depressing when nothing was going my way. Outside of Los Angeles, there were people my age who had marriages, mortgages, jobs, kids.

But not me. I was still basically a teenager.

Like April.

I returned to my apartment and showered the beach grit off my body. I put on a clean pair of underwear, then wrapped myself in my bathrobe, a green-and-white striped cotton number given to me by an ex-girlfriend who'd wisely listened to her friends' warnings about dating actors. I lit a candle and poured myself a heavy slug of Scotland's best. The single malt went down smooth and easy. I poured another. I long for those times when men knew how to drink.

I selected an old mystery novel and dropped into my reading chair. I love old books, not because I went to Harvard, but mostly because filmed entertainment bores me. I know too much about how the sausages are made, so to speak, and once you've experienced the backstage bullshit in that dream factory, it makes you nauseated to watch the final product.

Then my phone rang.

I decided to ignore it. I threw a towel over my head and concentrated harder on the story. It was already nine o'clock, too late for my reptilian agent to be calling. He was probably at his dinner table, sucking the bone marrow out of an infant. Truth be told, I didn't feel like being with humans anyways. There are times when a man needs to be alone, to build up the testosterone necessary to face the world.

The call went to voicemail, and there was blessed quiet for a little while. Then it began ringing again. I leaned over and looked at the display.

It was April Kim.

I froze. She had no business calling me. Not after our hand-to-hand combat. Not after the dwarf had pepper-sprayed me.

I let the call go to voicemail again. A minute later, it

rang a third time. There was no dissuading her. I finally picked up.

"What do you want?"

I had laid on the extra bitter sauce in my voice, but she didn't care. "Jake, please, if you care at all about me, don't hang up."

She sounded small, scared, and vulnerable. In the background I could hear commotion, shouting male voices, a heavy bass line. I felt a twinge of concern despite myself.

Still, this demand was ludicrous. "Maybe we ought to review the basics of negotiation," I said.

April skipped the fat and went straight for the meat. "Listen, I'm at a party. It's way out of control."

"Someone finds you entertaining enough to invite you to a party?"

"I need a ride home."

"So you need a cab."

There was a guilty silence. "It's just this once. I swear I won't ever ask again."

"Of course you won't, because you won't ever see me again."

I heard something shatter in the background, and she stumbled on her words as though they wouldn't leave her mouth. "I tried to apologize, you know, but you couldn't hear me."

"When I was unconscious on your porch? Sorry, go call Mina for a ride."

"She goes to sleep at eight."

"Don't you have any friends who drive?"

Exasperated, she spelled it out for me. "Listen. My parents think I'm *studying*."

The mist lifted from my brain. "Ah. So I'm both your ride *and* your excuse."

"Can you help me? This place is turning really scary."

Something snapped in me, and my patience evaporated into a cloud of steam. "Your maid freaking attacked me with *pepper spray* yesterday. After a fight that *you* instigated."

"So?"

"So I'm still flushing out my eyeballs every two hours."

"You could thank me. I stopped her from calling the cops."

"You're a saint."

Then she made an odd whimpering. I realized that April was crying. My eyeballs rolled so far backwards in my head that I could see myself thinking. What if this weren't an act? What if she really were distraught?

I sighed. "You're lucky I have a soft spot."

"You'll help me?" she said.

"Give me the address."

She repeated an address in Bell Canyon, and I wrote it down. I promised to be there in half an hour.

SIXTEEN

I stood up and wrapped my cotton robe more tightly around myself. I was comfortable and didn't want to leave. But the damsel-in-distress angle had worked. April had sunk her hooks into me.

I opened my closet and didn't like the looks of anything in it. Instead, I decided to wear my bathrobe. It was exactly how I felt. Besides, that would really stick it to April. I could really embarrass her if I left the car.

I slipped my wallet into the front pocket of the robe, put on my slippers, went down to my car, and left the neighborhood.

Under the high, hard crust of a crescent moon, I headed up the deserted Sepulveda Boulevard, over the hill into the San Fernando Valley. Immediately, the temperature spiked several degrees. Maybe it was from population. Two million people lived here now. A hundred years ago it had been almost empty.

I turned westwards, towards the lush gated neighborhoods of the western end. Leaving the freeway, I rolled down my window, soaking in the clean, wet smell of night-time greenery. I wound through arterial streets that had no sidewalks. That was because sidewalks didn't provide a solid return on investment.

Soon a gate loomed out of the darkness, and I rolled up to a brick guardhouse. Behind the window was a man wearing a blue uniform embroidered with the word *security*.

"Address?" he said.

I fumbled for my paper. "Eleven hundred Charing Cross Road."

"Name?"

"Doesn't matter. I'm just picking up a girl from a party."

He turned to me with a mixture of amusement and cunning on his face, like we were in on a secret together. "That's a high school party."

"I know."

The guard smirked. I could see the rear of my car on the closed feed monitor inside his booth, and suddenly I started to get paranoid. Maybe this was an elaborate setup. Maybe April was trying to sting me.

He asked my name again. No getting around this one. I spat it at him. Then he handed me a green paper with a date scribbled on it. "Put this on the dash. Two blocks up and left at the top of the hill." He paused. "Her parents'll be home in the morning."

"I'll be gone in ten minutes."

He smirked. "You're pretty quick. Better work on that."

I felt my patience leave me again. "You have something you want to say to me?"

"Better watch out," he replied, "or you could have a tow truck looking for you. We've got hidden ordinances you wouldn't believe."

Then he stopped talking. He was looking at me curiously. "Don't I know you from somewhere?" he said. "On television?"

He didn't deserve an answer. By now the gate had swung open. I floored my car through the open gate and sped into the community. This guardhouse nonsense was for the birds. The idea of an open, democratic community had been sold out. The people didn't want it. We were headed back to feudalism.

You could see why these people liked being walled off. The starter mansions were spaced generously on their lots, each decorated with expensive rock gardens and inter-locking pavers on the driveways. Classic white horse fences lined the road. Somewhere a mare whinnied.

At the top of the hill, I turned left and immediately spotted the party. It was a new Tudor that blazed with yellow light. Through the leaded glass windows, a sea of bodies bobbed and swelled. With the windows rolled down, I could hear the muted thumping of the music, the squeals of delight and rage and jealousy all the other extreme emotions of youth.

I waited outside the house with my engine idling. A gang of kids milled around the side door holding cigarettes awkwardly. They all ignored me. I laid on the horn, but that didn't do any good either.

Either April couldn't hear me, or she was in real trouble. After a few minutes I decided to find out.

I parked in a space far down the street, pulled the bathrobe around me tightly, and walked to the house. I knew what I would get. First there would be curious looks, then whispered mocking. That was fine. I liked playing the outsider. More than one casting director had seen that in me anyways.

I didn't bother to knock. I pushed my way inside the

foyer. The volume of the electronic dance music nearly pushed me back out.

At least eighty drunk people were going berserk in a vaulted-ceiling living room designed for no more than thirty. They sounded like a tribe of chimpanzees. In the corner, a pimply deejay behind a MacBook had one ear cocked into a pair of headphones.

The funny thing was that, beneath the party, the home had been decorated in an arts and crafts country style. There were red gingham checked throw pillows, wicker baskets, ceramic figurines.

I shambled through the adolescent bodies, nodding at eye contact, pretending to fit in. Girls swiftly jabbed elbows as I passed, leaning together in clumps and giggling.

I stood there for a minute, taking in the chaos. This was a teenage house party. I'd been to plenty. But it looked different now. I realized that I didn't miss those days.

There was no sign of April, but this was a big house, and she was small enough to be stuffed underneath a quarterback's armpit.

I moved into the kitchen. Empty tequila and vodka bottles sat in the wet countertop. A stack of red plastic party cups waited patiently nearby. A couple of girls leaned on each other for support by the kitchen table. One was trying to touch the back of a chair, but her hand kept missing.

The question needed to be short and direct. "Have you seen April Kim?"

The two looked at each other—and exploded in giggles.

"That was my first reaction too," I said.

"No, it's ... just...." one said.

They were laughing so hard now, one of them dropped onto the floor. They were holding hands.

"No, seriously ... stop. We have to answer him! She's, like up ... stairs ..."

That was the best I would get. The second girl literally fell on top of the first.

On my way upstairs, a skinny kid was hanging from the stairway banister. His long arm was extending, trying to grab the French chandelier that hung suspended over the marble foyer. I wanted to pound on his fingers wrapped around the railing. I had been in a foul mood to begin with, and this party was making it even worse.

In the upstairs hallway I discovered a gallery of doors. Most were locked from the inside—I didn't want to know why—but one was partly ajar. I knocked, then heard a familiar voice.

It was a spare bedroom. Inside, the only light was cast by a desk lamp. Under the light was a thick book. And hunched over the book was a silhouette of a slim girl.

It was April.

She was studying.

At a *party*.

"You're unbelievable," I said.

She jerked up. I peered around her and saw her close the cover. It was a thick book on social anthropology, by a professor. It'd won a Pulitzer Prize.

"It's extra credit for AP Human Geography." Then she checked her watch. "What took you so long?"

"I couldn't figure out what to wear."

She looked me up and down. "Nice one. White terrycloth would've made a stronger statement, though."

"You could just say thank you."

She looked at me uncomprehendingly. "You're getting paid."

I relaxed. That made the evening sting a little less. She

stood up, packed her bag, and went downstairs. I followed at a respectful distance. She said goodbye to a girl perched on the edge of a couch. The girl looked at me and twiddled her fingers goodbye to me.

I followed April outside, worried about what that damn security guard had said about tow trucks.

SEVENTEEN

My car was still there. April climbed into the passenger seat. From the look on her face, she could've been in the backseat of a manure truck.

"I know this isn't quite the luxury vehicle that you're used to," I said, starting the engine.

"No, it's not," she said.

As we rolled through the exit gate, the guard stepped out and stared menacingly. I narrowed my eyes back at him, then remembered that he couldn't see us.

I didn't have anything to say. I just drove, trying to ignore the small presence to my right. I felt her studying me.

"You have a good profile," she said suddenly.

"I'm flattered."

"If you keep being so sarcastic, we're never going to build a good relationship."

I looked at her. The comment was for real. Her face looked open, honest, and inquisitive.

I didn't respond. She sighed and looked out the window. Neither of us said anything for a couple of long minutes. There was no traffic this late, and I watched the arched streetlights pass over the car in rhythmic regularity. "That girl you said goodbye to. Is she a friend of yours?"

"Clarissa? Since forever. We know everything about each other."

"Tell me one secret about her," I said. She arched her eyebrows in response. "It's safe," I said. "You know I won't say anything."

She bought that. April curled her legs up underneath her, the way girls do when they feel secure enough to start gossiping. "Okay. Clarissa wears a wig. All her hair fell out mysteriously in the fourth grade. And it's *not* alopecia. She's been tested."

"Do her parents know about this party?"

"Of course."

"They're okay with it?"

She smirked. "They *supplied* it."

"Wow."

"Yeah. They're typical enablers."

"But your parents aren't okay with it?"

Her body tensed and her small hands flexed. "I don't know. My parents are just *freaks*. Haven't you ever known Koreans?"

"Not really."

She emitted an exasperated sigh. "They never relax. It's all about productivity. It doesn't matter what you actually do. They just care that you stay busy. Go to a Korean restaurant. You'll see women running around for ten minutes to deliver a single fork."

"You seem to be like that too."

She gave me another irritated stare. I was getting sick of those. "Please," she said. "I party *all* the time."

April said this without a trace of irony. I thought of the

silhouette in the bedroom, hunched over the book as the festivities raged below. It seemed that she lied to herself too.

Soon we descended the Sepulveda Pass, then turned west down Sunset, then floated back up the residential streets into the hills again. The curbs and mailboxes looked blurry, since the saltwater from the day's surfing had swollen and bleared my eyes. Plus it was almost eleven o'clock. I dreamed of eight hours in my fresh bedsheets.

"Don't park on the street," April suddenly said.

"I wasn't planning to park at all."

"I'll show you the hidden entrance instead. Turn left here."

She pointed towards an unmarked lane, concealed under a canopy of leafy branches. It wide enough for a single car. I turned into it.

The road turned into a narrow asphalt track that hugged the side of the mountain. My headlights cut across the scrub and manzanita that clung to the slope. To my left was a stunning view of the twinkling beach communities and the vast blackness beyond.

"What a dump," I said. "Seriously, how do you get any work done?"

"I've never really looked at the view," April said.

We arrived at a small iron gate similar to the one on the main street. There was a sleek callbox. On this one, however, I didn't see any numbers.

"Where do you punch the code?" I said.

"There is no code. It's biometric."

I sucked the inside of my cheek while April walked around the car, placed her finger on a sensor, and then returned. The gate slowly opened. I watched her cross the headlights. She didn't move like most teenagers, in fits and starts. No, her flat hips drove her body persistently forward.

We drove up the private driveway, lit by a line of antique gas lamps, through a stand of jack pines. In the orange glow of the lamps, they appeared healthy and robust. I thought that was weird. The bark beetle infestation had been ravaging conifers all over the southern part of the state. I would've asked April about it, but this was the end of the road.

The drive ended at the back end of the mansion, in a paved area settled in the vale between two hills. That explained why I hadn't seen it. On the asphalt someone had painted lines. A signpost driven into the ground read *Visitor Parking*.

"Where's the shuffleboard and buffet?"

"Funny. Listen, don't go yet."

"Why?"

She had pulled down the mirror on the visor and was using a Kleenex to wipe the lipstick and mascara from her face. "Because you have to come to the front door with me."

"No."

"But you *have* to. Mina won't let me in unless I'm with you."

"I thought she was in bed."

"No, she's waiting up. I called her."

My lip curled fiercely. This was feeling way too much like a date. More importantly, I didn't want to ever see that vicious little dwarf again.

"Why don't you just sneak in?" I said.

April folded her hands and looked very sad. She turned her head to the right and whispered something in such a small voice that I had to lean forward and cup my ear and ask her to repeat it.

"I don't have a key," she said.

"Why not?"

"They won't give me one." She looked up at me with a pale, sad face. "The front doors are always locked. This way they always know when I come home."

That was clever. Clever but cruel. A girl could grow up heartless in a home like that.

I turned the engine off and unbuckled my seatbelt. "Fine. Let's end this charade and we can both be on our merry ways."

April followed a small brick path to a side door of the mansion. It looked like a servant's entrance. I shuffled behind her in my bathrobe and didn't have to pretend to be casual. Maybe it was because of the hour. Maybe it was because I truly didn't care.

April put out a slim index finger and pressed the door-bell. The first joint of her finger bent unnaturally backwards. It didn't bother her. Sometimes girls seem so fragile that they could break. Then you think about childbirth and realize that women make us guys look like fruitcakes.

"Ten seconds," I said. "No more."

"I owe you," she said.

The doorbell sounded throughout the house. I thought about leaving this girl where she stood. But in the lintel above the door, a light flicked on. A deadbolt slid, and April immediately dropped her head in a subordinate position. It was like she'd suddenly assumed a character. Believe me, I know all about acting—and she had just started doing it.

The door swung open. The small humpback stepped out into the light. Her squid eye saw me and went as wide as a dinner plate. Her mouth grew ferocious.

Mina's hand scrambled in her pocket. If it was for the pepper spray canister, I wasn't waiting. I turned and flung myself into the nearby shrubbery. April quickly leapt onto the dwarf, explaining something in rapid Korean.

"You can come out," said April. "She's okay now."

I rose out of the turf cautiously. The servant had calmed down but the red flush of anger was still on her cheeks.

"Everything's okay here?" I said. "Great. Mina, good night. April, good night—and good luck. Have a nice life."

I swiveled on my heel and took off down the walk. I expelled a deep sigh of relief, knowing that I'd left this temperamental little overachiever behind forever.

Then a deep, unfamiliar voice said, "Mister Jake tutor."

I stopped and turned.

Standing in the doorway was the silhouette of a man, and something in his voice told me that this was April's father.

EIGHTEEN

I reluctantly staggered back toward the door, my head down, conscious of the man's eyes watching me.

As I approached, he stepped out into the porch light. He wore a black t-shirt, black silk slacks, and black sandals. His skin boasted that healthy sun-kissed brown tone that Asian men sometimes enjoy. But his almond eyes were pools of darkness, as black and inscrutable as an expert poker player's. They would betray nothing.

April said something quickly in Korean and gestured at me. His eyes flicked between us.

"You are my daughter's tutor," he said. He said it as though that fact had just surprised him. Then he suddenly stuck out his hand. I accepted it. That was my first mistake. He had a bone-crushing grip. I let out a small gasp.

"Mister Kim," I said, choking on the pain.

"Yes," he said. He let go of my hand. I stuck the wounded thing into my pocket to let it whimper in peace. "What keeps my daughter out so late?"

I hardly had the patience for this, and my face showed it.

"He was helping me study," April said.

Her father looked surprised. "In a bathrobe?"

One thing you should know about me is that, on occasion, I am capable of tremendous bullshitting. So I swung for the fences.

"It makes my students feel comfortable," I said.

"To wear a bathrobe?"

"Yes. I wear it every day. It's my work outfit."

I held his gaze. Half of successful lying is confidence. He was poised on the brink of disbelief.

Then a light began to glow in those dark almond eyes, and a big smile spread into his sharp cheeks. "You are funny, Jake tutor," he said.

"So I've been told."

"You must stay for dinner."

"At this hour?"

He smiled. "I just came home from a business trip. I am hungry."

I really wanted to say no. But understand that I'm a bachelor. Understand that surfing stokes an appetite like nothing else. And the pathetic ham and mustard sandwich waiting for me at home couldn't compete with the pungent scent of Korean barbecue wafting from beyond.

"You're the boss, so I accept," I said.

I waited for an apologetic glance from April, but she just flitted inside without acknowledging me. It seemed that her dad didn't know anything about our fight. Or about pepper spray. Or about my quitting the job.

I kicked off my slippers before the dwarf could spray me again. I entered the kitchen of the Kim mansion.

NINETEEN

The kitchen was expansive and impeccably clean. The décor was walnut wood with silver accents. A woman who I hadn't seen before was busy working over steaming iron pots and sizzling pans.

At a long, low table, a small Korean feast awaited us. Small bowls of appetizers had been laid out in porcelain cups. There were bean sprouts, bean cakes, and kimchi.

April threw her book bag into a corner and took a seat at the table. "You can sit here," she said, gesturing beside her.

"No," her father said, "he sits next to me."

"Haven't we sat next to each other enough tonight?" I said to her. "All that studying?"

April's little mouth opened and closed. She couldn't say anything to that without entering the land of the liar. It was a masterful setup. I dutifully slid into the seat to her father's right.

The family immediately set into the food. Their chopsticks were a blur, shoveling bits of sticky white rice and barbequed ribs from plate to mouth. Nobody spoke. April cast nervous glances at me and her father.

The food was good. I finished first. Her father finished second and dropped his chopsticks onto his plate. He swung his arms back and laced his hands behind his head. A small burp crawled out of his mouth like an insect. His eyes were watery and slack.

Then he swung his head around towards me. His eyes grew unfocused and gazed above and beyond me as if he were figuring out a vague shape in a distant cloud.

"So much food," he said. "So much house. So many *things*. I am worried, Mister Jake tutor." His eyes swam towards me. "I am worried that my daughter is becoming spoiled."

April lowered her head and stared hard into her plate.

I played the go-between. "She's got a good head on her shoulders."

He looked at me for a moment, thinking about that as if nobody had ever mentioned it to him. I felt myself getting nervous. It was easy to feel intimidated around him.

Then his monologue continued. "I was born in a small village near Pusan. Later, when I get older, the people in Seoul make fun of me. For my accent. For always eating kimchi. Breakfast, lunch, dinner. Even though they do the same. Now look at me." He gestured around. "Big shot."

"That's right," I said. "BMOC."

It meant Big Man On Campus, but he didn't know that. I could tell because he ignored it. April's father was the type of man who would ignore something rather than admit that he didn't know anything.

"I think my children are spoiled," he repeated. Then he looked at me as though he had just remembered something vitally important. "We have three BMWs. And a Mercedes. Why we have so many?"

I faked a casual yawn. "Maybe sell one."

This tickled him. A booming laugh exploded from the bottom of his soul. "You know, April doesn't drive."

"I know."

"I mean, she has a driver. Like a rich girl."

April wasn't *like* a rich girl, she *was* a rich girl. Meanwhile, a smug expression had slathered itself on her father's face. He was an odd duck. If he had problems with his wealth, I knew lots of people willing to relieve him of some of it.

Meanwhile, April had stopped eating. Her neck muscles were strained tensely as she stared into her dish. She wouldn't make eye contact. I was kind of glad that I'd come inside. It was good to see her humbled.

Mina cleared dishes and brought new ones. Nobody paid her any attention. My eyeballs quivered whenever she passed behind me.

Her father began thundering again. "You know, there is something else about this country." He narrowed his eyes. "Drugs! So many drugs! So easy to find!" He turned to April. "You start with drugs—"

"—and you'll send me to Korea," she finished, "where nobody ever uses drugs."

"Nobody."

I decided to throw her a bone. "What else can't you do?"

"I can't go down to the factory or I'll get mugged."

Her father grew more agitated. "It's in East LA. Very bad neighborhood." He addressed me too. "April don't know about life. She think every place like Bel Air."

April was barely holding onto the act. I could see her small fists clenching and unclenching. "I've traveled to thirty-nine countries, Jake."

I realized that I'd become a lightning rod for this family's angst. It wasn't fun. My stomach was full. I was tired. I needed an exit strategy.

Suddenly I was aware of April's father. He was staring at me with new, shrewd eyes. "So, Mister Jake tutor. You have been tutor a long time?"

The hell with it. I would tell him the truth. "Not really."

His face darkened. "You have been successful in another field before this?"

"Sure—if you count wearing a kilt and pretending to be a Scottish exchange student with a taste for bestiality." It had been one of my plummiest roles, playing comic relief in a direct-to-video slasher movie. I'd been terrible.

Mister Kim looked at me blankly, so I explained it. "I used to be an actor."

Nothing registered on his face. I guessed that anything creative or expressive would be met with this same response. "Mister Jarvis says he only hire the best tutors," he said.

"He does."

A cunning look appeared at the corner of his mouth. "Mister Jake tutor, I need to know something else."

I could tell this was the crisis point. "Shoot."

"What university did you go to?"

April was looking at me. Even Mina had sensed the temperature change. She'd slung a towel over her shoulder and cast a fishy eye towards me.

They were all waiting for the answer. I wasn't too naïve to realize that this was the ultimate moment of approval for a Korean family. It was time to drop the H-bomb.

"Harvard," I said.

April dropped her chopsticks. "Liar," she said.

"I'm not lying."

"You're *such* a liar."

"Why would I lie to you?" I protested. "Ask Jarvis. We were classmates."

"Are you serious?" she said. "I mean, you're smart, but you don't seem *that* smart. No offense."

"None taken."

"You play sports?" her father asked.

"No."

"Legacy?" she said.

I shook my head. "Some people go to community college, some people go to state universities. I went to Harvard." I shrugged and popped another piece of barbequed meat into my mouth. I was happy, casual, and clueless. The same act I always put on whenever dropping the H-bomb.

Mr. Kim was a sight to see. His jaw jutted out. He seemed to grow bigger and his guts seemed to swell inside his body. Then he shrunk down. His eyes suddenly couldn't meet my own.

"It is an honor to have you in my home, Mister Jake tutor," he said.

"Thank you."

April's tongue was probing her cheek as she gazed at me with new eyes. The Kims didn't know how dangerously close they were approaching to my second secret, the one I never tell anybody.

But that didn't matter, because soon the plates were cleared away, and Mister Kim's friendly hand was on my back, guiding me down the hall.

TWENTY

It was a mystery to me how wearing a bathrobe could put other people at ease. Maybe because it suggested a harmless insouciance, a devil-may-care attitude. I resolved to wear it the next time I went out to the bars.

April's father kept touching the robe, saying "bathrobe" to himself. He really liked the damn thing.

Meanwhile, he led me into the private study. It felt like it was trying too hard. A pair of heavy doors opened into a chamber that had sprung from the imagination of a British aristocrat. At one end were leaded glass windows. At the other was a pair of leather couches with studded with bronze rivets at the seams. A sea of thick pile carpeting lapped at the edges of the room. In the corner stood an imposing safe that looked it could withstand a team of Soviet safecrackers.

"Too many things," her father muttered. For no reason he swatted a candelabra that rested on the lintel above the fireplace. It crashed to the floor.

"Mister Kim—" I began.

He interrupted with an impatient wave of his hand. "No Mister. Now you call me Jae Woo."

He headed over to a side table and screwed open a green bottle and poured a clear liquid into two glasses. He handed me one.

"This is the most popular drink in Korea," Jae Woo said. "For men like me. And you."

I sipped it hesitantly. It tasted like vodka with a touch of tapioca.

"Soju," he said. "If you don't like it, get out."

"I don't like it."

"Are you telling me the truth?"

"No."

He laughed loudly, a big bark. "About *every*thing?"

"What does that mean?" I said.

In an instant, Jae Woo had taken the soju out of my hands, spun me around, and placed my hands against the wall. It all happened before I could react. His hands felt along the sides of my body, on my chest, and on my back.

Then he spun me forwards again and grabbed the lapel of my bathrobe. He looked into my eyes. His pupils were small, intense chips of coal. I noticed his thuggish muscled arms. I felt more nervous than during Mina's attack.

"Is everything okay?" I said.

This must've satisfied him, because he relaxed his grip. I smoothed my bathrobe, plunged one hand into the pocket, held my drink with the other, and pretended to play it cool. I was an actor. I convinced myself that this was just a scene.

I walked to a family photograph hanging on the wall. A three-year-old April was clothed in colorful traditional Korean attire. An older girl wore a pinched look on her face and stared defiantly into the lens. I get a sixth sense about people sometimes, and it was telling me that this girl wasn't happy.

"That's Hwi Won, my oldest daughter," he said. "She went to Stanford."

"That's a good school."

"It's not Ivy League."

"So what?"

"In Korea they announce on television the students going to Ivy League school."

Jae Woo fell into one of the couches. I did the same in the couch opposite. The leather cushions were at least a foot deep.

"Mister Jake tutor, I want to ask you a question," he said.

"Okay," I said.

"How is April doing?"

I held my drink up to the light and clinked the ice cubes. My voice sounded lazy. "Your daughter is extremely talented and deserves everything she gets."

He shook his head. "No. I want you to tell me the truth. How is she *doing*?"

"She's doing fine."

Jae Woo emitted an exasperated sigh. "That's not true."

It was time to try a different tack. "Okay," I said, "if you want to know the truth, April *sucks*."

He smiled, and that's when I knew I'd struck gold. My mouth kept going.

"She's a horrible student," I said, "the very worst."

Her father leaned forward on the couch, a wicked grin decorating his skull. "You know, sometimes she make very stupid comments."

"I can't believe you would raise such an idiot," I said.

He laughed again, harder this time, a staccato *rat-a-tat-*

tat sound like an automatic weapon. "Once she say to me, 'Daddy, what's four plus five?' I play trick and say 'forty-five'. She say, 'Oh, okay, Daddy!' So *stupid!*"

Jae Woo's eyes bulged with laughter and he clutched his stomach. "Forty-five!" he said again. Laughter rolled across his body.

I tried to control my facial expression. This guy was a bona fide asshole. Still, I always ride the horse in the direction it's going, so I dug up the momma jokes that another actor had entertained me with between takes on an after-school special.

"Do you know how stupid April is?" I said.

"How stupid?"

"April is so stupid," I said, "she thought that a quarterback was a refund."

Jae Woo slapped his knee. "Yes! Yes!"

"April is so stupid she spent two hours staring at a glass of orange juice because it had *concentrate* written on the package."

"Ha ha ha—"

"April is so stupid, I don't know whether to call the Guinness people or cut off her head and fill it with geraniums!"

The convulsions abruptly stopped, and he rocketed to his feet with a stone-cold expression on his face. His nostrils flared. Perhaps I'd crossed a line with that last one. I braced for an attack.

Instead, he said, very calmly and intensely: "I like you, Mister Jake tutor. Very much."

"I like you too, Jae Woo."

"I'm going to give you a gift," he said.

He left the room for a moment, and I could hear him ordering something urgently to Mina. I adjusted the belt of my bathrobe and wondered how much longer this torture was going to last.

Two minutes later they returned. The dwarf was carrying a pink box in her outstretched hands. She passed it to me, nodded respectfully, and left the room.

Jae Woo said, "I am very tired now. Please have a good night, Mister Jake tutor." He dipped his head to me before leaving. That was a sign of respect.

I blinked helplessly. The abrupt departure left me stunned. I was alone, in my bathrobe, on the couch, in Jae Woo's private study, with a pink box on my lap. The situation was telling me to open the lid.

I did so. Inside was a white bean mung cake. It was a popular dessert among Koreans. It looked pretty.

Then I noticed what seemed to be paper peeking from beneath the cake. I tugged on the corner gently. It was an envelope.

I pulled it all the way and cleaned off the envelope with the enclosed napkins. Then I opened.

Inside was money. It was a short stack, but they were big denominations.

This was a bribe.

TWENTY-ONE

Suddenly I realized what had happened here. Jae Woo had probably known all along that I'd already ditched April. In fact, it was possible that he'd arranged for April to conveniently get ditched at the party, but that was just speculation.

In any case, he should've had an Oscar.

I started to count the money, then stopped. It was too much. If I accepted this bribe, I could really kiss off the Earthen Jug, at least for a while. But doing so would mean spending more time with this gifted, unstable banshee of a teenager. An apple that hadn't fallen too far from its tree.

When I stepped into the hallway with the pink box tucked under my arm, the house had fallen dark and silent. I used my fingertips to feel my way along the wall, like a sane patient sneaking out from a lunatic asylum.

In the kitchen, I placed the box on the table. Then I gently placed the envelope on top. This bribe wasn't enough. I was truly finished with this family.

My hand was on the doorknob when April's voice sounded from the shadows. "How much did he offer you?"

I paused. She stepped out of the darkness. She was wearing a pair of long-sleeved black pajamas that cloaked everything but her moonish face.

"A lot," I said. "I stopped counting at a thousand."

"He gave the last guy five hundred."

"Liar."

She shifted her weight to the opposite foot. The sign of the disingenuous.

"You'd better not toy with me," I said. "My self-esteem is already in the basement."

"Now you're lying."

"Why do you think I'm always lying?"

"There aren't any basements in this state."

"We can banter for hours if it makes you feel better about yourself. Me, I'd rather just go home and sleep."

"I never would've guessed you went to Harvard," she said. "You're not arrogant enough."

"See," I said, "that's what Ivy League schools do, ironically. They take all the piss and vinegar out of you. Everybody there has already been told they're one in a million. So everybody voluntarily lays down their arms, because otherwise it's mutually assured destruction of egos." I paused. "Maybe you should try it some time."

She ignored that. "If I said that we ought to keep working together, how would you respond?"

I looked coolly at her.

"Why are you so hooked on having me as a tutor?" I said. "There are dozens of other people who could help you."

Her voice broke a little, and she became girlish and petulant. "Because I want what *you've* got."

"A nagging uncertainty about your place in the universe?"

"No. A degree from Harvard."

Of course she wanted the Ivy sheepskin. Her zip code was packed full of brand whores. I'd already noticed the purple Balenciaga handbag in her study. It cost as much as the gross domestic product of a small African nation.

"And you, Jake," she said, nodding to the envelope, "I know that *you* want what *we* have."

God, she was right. I lowered my head. I would knuckle under, cry uncle, sign on the dotted line. I was selling my soul again, but at least it would be short-term.

I stuffed the envelope into my bathrobe. "You can keep the cake."

"I'll have Mina serve it to us tomorrow."

"Usual time?"

She nodded. "I'll let Jarvis know. He's going to be so stoked. He's been harassing me to get you back all week."

Of course Jarvis would be excited. As I left the house, I felt a tickle in my stomach—and it told me that the excitement was only beginning.

TWENTY-TWO

To my surprise, April swallowed her attitude and bore down on the work.

Jarvis had instructed me to focus entirely on the SAT, since the test date was only three weeks away. So I barely stayed ahead of her, studying the questions each afternoon before driving up into the hills to tame my small tigress with a whip and a stool.

One afternoon, after finishing a set of simultaneous equations, she tossed down her pen. "I am sick of this," she announced.

"But you're doing a good job," I said.

"I've been doing these stupid questions for almost *four years.*"

She bit into the pear that Mina had served us on a chilled plate. It'd been peeled, sliced, and punctured with toothpicks—the traditional Korean way.

"Maybe you should take a break," I said. "Do something fun and normal."

"What do you like to do?"

"I surf."

She nodded. "I've always wanted to try that."

"You're welcome to join me. I go right by the Hermosa Beach pier. I'm usually there on weekend mornings."

"I don't know," she said. "Surfing is just so relaxing. There's no point."

"You know," I replied, "having no point kind of *is* the point. Not everything you do has to be for a trophy."

"Maybe."

I decided to switch back to academics. "How are classes going?"

"Ridiculously busy," she said. "I have a paper due on Friday. I don't have the time to write it."

"Tell me more about it."

She sighed. "Ten pages on Edward Jenner and the milk-maid theory."

"I haven't heard of that. It sounds interesting."

A strange look clouded her face, and she spoke out of the left side of her mouth. "Jake, maybe you'd like to help me."

"How so?"

"I've checked out all the research." She gestured to a pile of books. "If I give it to you, do you think it could get written?"

Like government officials, she was using the passive voice to hide responsibility. The truth was, I had felt this offer coming. Tutors have been writing rich kids' papers ever since tutors and rich kids were invented. Still, I'd expect this offer from an effete drug addict. I hadn't expected this offer from *her*—the overachieving, micro-managing, control-freak April Kim.

"I'd have to know the assignment first."

She reached over and handed me an envelope. I removed the paper inside. It was a photocopy of the assignment, already prepared for me. The brazenness of her manipulation was astounding.

"It's worth an extra grand," she said. "My dad okayed it."

"This is totally wrong."

"It's not that I can't do it," she said. "I could probably write this paper better than you. I just don't have *time*."

I had to admit that she was right. This wasn't a matter of motivation. This was a matter of priorities. I could argue that maybe she shouldn't have overloaded her schedule with so many advanced classes—so many, in fact, that she'd been forced to drop lunch. It was true. April fed herself like a horse from a bag of dry cereal between classes.

But tutors can't tell students to slack off. We're on the other side. We're expected to crack the whip harder, demand better insights, mock the need for sleep—despite the fact that many teenagers are hormonally incapable of forming coherent sentences before ten o'clock am. I was actually helping her achieve her dreams.

At least that's how I rationalized it as I piled the books into my car and drove home.

TWENTY-THREE

For the next two days I forgot that I had ever been an actor.

Instead I plunged into a whole new area of thought, the world of professors who squint at maps and devise statistics about protein yield in various ancient grains. There was a lot to learn in the field of evolutionary geography.

The milkmaid theory stated that the European standard of female beauty was equated with good health—all because someone noticed that pretty milkmaids lived longer than other women. It turns out that sitting at the rear end of a cow all day leads to exposure to pathogens, which builds up one's immune system. Milkmaids were known for their clear complexions and robust health, all because they had the immune system to survive massive blasts of cow fart.

It's crazy. I'll stop talking about it. You can look it up for yourself.

By noon on Thursday I'd printed out the ten-page headache. I was sitting at my laptop poring through apartment rentals. Nothing was available for less than $700 per month. Then my phone rang. It was April Kim.

"Tell me it's done," she said.

I glanced towards my desk. "Hot off the laser jet."

"I need it by seventh mod."

"Today?"

"Yeah. I had the date wrong. Actually, my teacher changed it."

"How uncharacteristic of you. I'll email it."

"There's no time," she said. "Can you bring it here in an hour?"

"You can't go to the computer lab and print it out?"

"They won't allow me during class."

I sighed. She was treating me like hired help again. It was hard to tell if the demands came from the Korean side or the rich side.

"I want two hundred more," I said, then hung up the phone without waiting for an answer. It would be the most expensive courier service in her lifetime. That's how you negotiate with extortionists.

TWENTY MINUTES up Coldwater Canyon lay the famous Chandler-Beacon Preparatory School. It was nestled just below Mulholland Drive, high above the city in the Santa Monica Mountains. Occupying forty-four acres of the most overvalued property in the world, the place looked like an all-inclusive Barbados resort. It had the whitewashed walls, the sharply manicured green athletic fields, the marble walkways, the stylish on-campus townhouses for faculty.

I didn't feel like explaining myself to the guard to the visitor parking, so I dropped my car on a nearby side street and managed to slip around the guardhouse on foot. Under my arm was tucked the manila folder with the paper, as discreet as possible. It felt like contraband.

I veered towards an open-air courtyard cloaked with bougainvillea. A few kids lazed around an aluminum table that shone blindingly in the midday sun.

"Where's the office?" I said.

A boy lifted his hooded lizard eyes to me. They hinted at a future in human dismemberment. Slowly his arm pointed towards the front gate.

The others giggled. "Tory, you're a douche," said one.

I stood there staring down at an unbroken circle of thin hunched shoulders and shaggy heads. "All right," I said, "different question. Do you know where April Kim is?"

They exploded into giggles. One voice asked, "How old are you?"

That one stung, but I brushed it off. "Her name is April Kim. She's a senior. Petite Asian."

They looked at each other and that inside joke erupted again. I gave up and moved on.

I also gave up on the idea of finding the office. It just wasn't smart on an illicit mission such as this. My movements would have to be under the table.

Walking down a breezy corridor, I noticed a bulletin announcing "working vacations" to Rome, Zurich, and Fiji for five grand each. Another bulletin announced that the stained-glass studio would be only open until five pm starting on Monday. A third advertised the fact that next Thursday would be Prada Day, part of something called Fall Fashion Celebration.

I felt a chill run down my spine. This wasn't normal. This was worlds away from the flat-roofed prison chamber that'd dumped a high school diploma on me. I wasn't entirely sure that it was any better, either.

On the other side of the courtyard was a partly open door. A sign read Office of Student Government. That was promising. I could slip in under the noses of the adults.

I crossed the courtyard, gave a quick courtesy knock, then pushed into the room.

TWENTY-FOUR

A slender kid in skinny jeans lay stretched out on a couch, facing away from me. One knee jutted up in the air, and his hands were laced behind his head. He was lazily tapping the touchscreen of a very expensive tablet.

"Hey," I said.

"Tickets for the Friday capoeira festival go on sale after second mod tomorrow," he said, without looking.

"I'm not a student."

He twisted his neck around so he was looking at me almost upside down. "You're not a teacher."

"I'm just looking for somebody."

Sighing, he hoisted himself to a sitting position and ran an aggravated hand through his hair. He flicked shut the cover on the tablet with a mean finger.

"Why don't you just go to the office?" he said.

"Maybe I don't want to talk to them. Maybe I want to talk to you."

Not a single eyelash twitched. He crossed his arms and just looked at me. A puddle of attitude pooled at his feet.

"Do you have a name?" I said.

"Not for you."

"Then I'll just call you head altar boy."

"I'm Jewish," he replied.

"The girl is named April Kim," I said. "Petite Asian, senior. Do you know her?"

He stood up and walked over to the window. He cracked it open, then pulled an e-cigarette off its charger in the wall. His lips wrapped around the device, and he stood there puffing silently. This whole act was for me—as though it were my privilege to witness his flaunting his defiance of school rules.

"You've got to be *kidding* me," he finally said.

For the fortieth time that day I felt as though I'd just uttered the most buffoonish comment possible. Rich, shrewd teenagers have a way of making you feel useless.

"I feel like we're having a communication problem," I said.

"Everybody's feelings are valid," he said.

"Did your shrink tell you that?"

"Your mother did."

"Drop it," I warned, "you've never met my mother."

"I wouldn't want to," he said.

"I wouldn't want you to either," I said. "She's been dead for five years."

Unembarrassed, he just snorted. "You've got a quick mouth."

"Funny, they said I was slow when I was here."

His eyebrows lifted. "You went to Chandler?"

"Graduated top of the class." It wasn't true, but if you need to lie, then go big.

A cunning look sharpened his features. "Was Mister Tachardski a total cock when you were here too?"

"How long's he been here?"

"Damn, like thirty years. The guy's part of the scenery."

These clubby types drive me bonkers with their head games. I stared the kid straight in the eyes. "Mister Tachardski doesn't exist. You made him up."

It was a bold guess—and it paid off. He hung his head with a guilty look. "All right," he said.

"Are you ready to help me now?"

"I'm Sam," he said, sticking his hand out, "senior class president. I know everybody and everything here. Except for why you would want to meet April Kim."

I shook his hand, which was thin and cold. "If you'd said that earlier," I said, "this conversation could've been a lot nicer."

"This isn't a public service," he said, yawning. "I've just got an open mod."

"Tell me about April. What happened? She steal your birthday cupcake?"

He got suspicious. "Why do you want to know?"

"I'm her tutor." He'd cocked his head sideways, so I reassured him of my indifference. "Don't worry, she's nothing to me—a piece of plaster."

The kid nodded as though he'd expected exactly those words. It was irritating. He'd probably learned to nod to avoid the appearance of losing control.

"So that bitch ran against me for president last year," the kid said. He was getting more amped up. "She started a whisper campaign that I got some girl pregnant over at Pali."

"I won't say anything."

He made a *pffft* sound and swiped the air with his hand like a conductor. "I don't care. She knows I hate her. *Everybody* hates her."

"It's hard to like someone who's so competitive."

"I'm competitive too."

"My point exactly," I said.

He flipped me off. Then he glanced at his watch and replaced his e-cigarette in the charger.

"She doesn't take a lunch," I explained.

The kid smirked again. "April doesn't take a lunch because she'd face total and complete isolation in the dining hall if she entered it. Have you met her dad?"

I nodded.

"That dude is *shady*. I heard that he owned a grip of sweatshops near downtown. Makes little migrant kids sew buttons and shit."

This was news to me. From the hallway there sounded a soft tone, a melodious tinkle, followed by a murmur of voices. That had been the school bell. The mod had ended.

"Do you know where I can find her?"

He slung his backpack over his shoulders. "She's in McGarry's AP Bio lab until fifth mod."

"You really *do* know everyone and everything."

"It's my business." He grinned like a future lobbyist. "Follow me. I'll show you the way."

TWENTY-FIVE

I followed Sam through the swarms of overdressed teens. The faces reflected the new nation forming on the coasts of our old nation. The standby white and black faces were there, but so were Chinese, Korean, Filipino, Ethiopian, Russian, Persian, Jewish—even Persian Jewish.

Meanwhile, Sam was gladhanding everybody who passed. Under his breath, he kept up a running narration for my benefit: "That chick's dad just got sent to prison for tax evasion. That guy got busted for using a prostitution ring. And see that baller? His dad signed Jay-Z."

Then he pulled me over to an alcove. "Do you have your phone?"

"Yeah."

He opened his own. It was a top-of-the-line device that was so new that I didn't even recognize it. He scrolled down the contact list. "So there's this guy Thad. He was my personal trainer for lacrosse last year, and he trained April too. Some crazy stuff went down between them. If you want to really find out dirt about her, this dude owns the freaking dump truck."

I didn't really want more dirt, but that made sense. Entering the Kim mansion, I would need all the information possible, so I copied Thad's number into my phone. But I didn't thank the kid, because it would've fueled his ego.

Then he pointed to an open door in a corner. "That's the bio lab."

"Glad you decided to trust me," I said.

"You've got a way about you," he said. "You don't seem, like, angry or weird."

"I'm also an actor," I answered.

Sam tipped his chin, and his upper lip curled slightly. He had a problem with authority. I looked forward to reading about his indictment someday.

Then he disappeared, and I didn't watch him go. Instead, I hustled over to the doorway to the biology laboratory and peered around the edge. Students in white lab coats gathered in clumps around the tables. The smell of formaldehyde crinkled my nose.

April wasn't hard to find. She was using a long pair of calipers to turn something dead in a dish. Three lab partners stood around her, their faces a mixture of boredom and resentment. When one tried to help, she elbowed him swiftly.

The queen bee.

I waved idiotically, trying to get her attention. The folder felt heavy against my ribcage.

"What do you need?" a voice said.

It belonged to a middle-aged man, also in a white coat, who was now standing between us. His face had the wary look that plasters the face of any teacher who feels in over his head.

"I don't need anything. April told me to come by here."

"During *my* lab?"

"Yes," I said.

"Where's your visitor's badge?" he said, eyeing my shirt. "Did you visit the office?"

Then the sinister voice of an angel interrupted us. It was April. She'd seen me and sprinted over. "Mister McGarry," she complained, "Steve is being so uncooperative. I have to do everything."

He wasn't deterred. "April, who is this person asking for you?"

"He's nobody," she said.

I nodded. "Yep. A human zilch."

The instructor looked unconvinced, so she extended the bullshit. "He's a messenger from my dad's company. What do you have for me?"

Well played, I thought. This would be fun. "Well," I said, "these are the application forms your dad told you about. The deadline is tomorrow." I looked at the teacher. "They've got to be signed and postmarked by this afternoon."

April motioned at her lab partners, who were now punching each other's shoulders with increasing intensity. "Can you go talk to them, Mister McGarry? I can handle this."

Keeping an eye on me, the teacher moved off. As soon as he was out of earshot, I congratulated her. "You must be running out of little fingers to twist people around."

"McGarry does as he's told," she answered. "Let's go outside."

She took my arm and propelled me outside, into the same alcove that Sam had pulled me into. I started to make a big show of the handover, but she snatched the folder from my arm.

"It's everything you ever wanted," I said.

She scanned the pages, nodding. "This is acceptable."

"Of course it is," I said.

"Thank you," she said.

Then April handed the folder back to me. Her face was blank and betrayed no emotion.

"April, this is *your* paper. I drove here just to give it to you."

"Yes, you did. And I appreciate the effort."

"But you're giving it back to me."

"Yes."

"You don't want it?"

"No, I don't."

"Why not?"

"I already wrote my own."

My tongue went drier than a sand dune. A sheen of sweat sprung out on my lower back.

"What?" I croaked.

"I already wrote my own."

"If you already wrote the paper, why did you ask me to do it?"

She flashed a wicked grin. "To see if you would."

"Which I did."

"Yes."

I started to see the outlines now. "Okay—but tell me what that means. That I take orders?"

"It means you can be trusted again."

At first I was shocked, but only for a moment. The truth was that I was tired of reacting. I'd been played like Starcraft by two teenagers in the same day. I was just sick of it.

I heard the words come flying out of my mouth. "You're a manipulative bitch."

She lifted her palms to the ceiling. "I had to test you. You quit on me. The first one *ever*, by the way."

At least she didn't deny the manipulative part. That meant there still dwelled within her a speck of self-awareness. I started to walk away, then turned back, then walked away, then turned back again.

"I'm still getting paid," I said.

"You will if you're still helping me."

I couldn't look at her. My eyes felt like they were brimming with hot fluid that would leak out if I did.

"Fine."

"Fine," she answered. "Take the afternoon off. I'll see you tomorrow."

Then something switched in her. A big authentic smile spread across her face. She skipped lightly back into the laboratory. A lighthearted girl once more.

I stood watching the door, wondering just how much longer it would be before I found a way to take control of this relationship.

TWENTY-SIX

In my car, I opened my phone and stared at the new name on the list of contacts. *Thad*.

There was no real need to call the personal trainer. I didn't need more dirt on April. It was wiser to follow a modern-day Monroe Doctrine. Avoid entangling alliances. Keep head down, say nothing, stay in the middle of the pack.

But the temptation to meddle was too great. I swallowed the red pill and dialed Thad's number. A man's voice answered on the second ring: "Holistic Health."

"I need to talk to Thad," I said.

"You've got him," the voice trilled. It was as flamboyant as a pair of nipple tassels.

"Are you available for a personal training session?"

He giggled. "It depends on who's calling."

I spotted an empty can of soda in the footwell of my car. "Frankie Fanta," I said.

"Well, Frankie Fanta, you have a *fabulous* name."

"So people tell me."

"What kind of training do you need?"

He'd caught me off guard. "Whatever you'd like to offer," I said. Too late I realized what that sounded like to a man of his persuasion.

Thad made a weird explosive snort, like a lid rattling as it struggled to contain the contents of a boiling pot.

"Oh God. Listen, Mister Law, I do *not* do that anymore. How did you get this number?"

I sighed. "Thad, I'm not a police detective or a pervert. I just need someone to motivate me to exercise."

"Well, I've got December fourteenth at eleven a.m."

"How generous. Only six weeks away."

"I'm the best."

"Can I tell you something else?"

"If you must."

"Sam at Chandler–Beacon recommended you."

I heard him pause. Sometimes I can hear different types of pauses over the phone line—bored pauses, scared pauses, interested pauses, guarded pauses. This was a significant pause. "*Really*. What time are you looking to meet?"

"Any time this week."

"I have today at two o'clock."

So Sam was the grease that would slide me into Thad's little world. "Can you let me know your rates?" I said.

"My rate is get here by two o'clock. Do you know where my studio is?"

"No."

"Pencil and paper."

He gave me the address, and soon I pointed my car towards West Hollywood.

NINETY YEARS AGO, West Hollywood was a hick town, wide fields dotted with bungalows, orchards, and the occasional roadside speakeasy—far enough from downtown for police not to bother busting up.

In the years that followed, the fields were replaced with row after dense row of two-story dingbat apartment complexes. The scrubby land paved over with hot, hard, urban asphalt.

Today, it's got the largest concentration of homosexuals in southern California, along with a smattering of Russian immigrants. I'll never understand that alliance. But what's more memorable to me is its three-quarters scale. Everything feels like it was built in miniature—the houses, alleys, parking spots, schnauzers, pinky fingers.

But no children. I'd never seen so much as a tricycle wheel within a mile of its borders. It was just as well, for at the end of the twentieth century West Hollywood had become a bizarre land of junkies, dope fiends, sadsacks, predators, and impoverished producers' assistants.

A weird knocking in the engine accompanied me on the drive. I tacked a mental note to bring the car into my mechanic.

I drove eastwards on Santa Monica Boulevard, past La Cienega, past Crescent Heights. Then I saw the address and parallel parked my car into a tight spot. This was a blessing. Parking spots on Santa Monica are rarer than virgins here.

I fed the meter with change scrounged up from my cup holder, then stood on the sidewalk and took it all in. Muscular men with shaved heads and tight sleeveless shirts sashayed past. They smelled like oiled muscles and male cologne.

Moving down the boulevard, I ignored a couple of

sailors leering at me from a coffee shop. I found Thad's studio on the second floor of a building, squinched between an environmentally friendly dry cleaner and a popular thrift store that offered free HIV tests.

The door was just a black iron thing with a simple number over the top. Nothing else to note its presence. The celebrity sensor in my head started to beep quietly.

I pulled the door open and found a set of iron stairs lined with expensive matte-finish sconces on the walls. At the top was another door, a vintage number made of perfectly distressed wood and iron brackets placed just so. It was Gothic industrial chic.

This was the verification I needed. Thad's business catered to the one percent—and they always reveal themselves in textures.

I hiked up the stairs and went through the door.

TWENTY-SEVEN

Thad's fitness studio was a yellow sunlit room with beautiful bamboo floors. A ballet barre was bolted into a mirror along the far wall. There was an array of pastel rubber mats at one end. The room smelled of vanilla floor polish. The sound of muted traffic hummed on the boulevard below.

In the middle of the room was a woman on the floor, lying on her back on a yoga mat. She was balancing a large green bouncy ball in the cradle formed by her crotch and inner thighs.

Above her, a rangy, limber man in a yellow cutoff t-shirt and red velour track pants was bent over the ball. She hoisted the ball up with her hips, and he thrust down upon the ball with his hips.

Hoist, thrust, hoist, thrust.

"Work it," he said. I recognized the voice as Thad's.

"I *am* working it," she said.

"Wait for the burn."

"God, this feels *way* too familiar."

"Speak for yourself," he said, humping her again.

I stood against the wall with my arms folded until he noticed me. Then the bizarre coitus quickly ended. He rolled off the ball, and her butt crashed to the floor. "Good job today," he said. "You'll bring Mandy next time?"

"I don't know, she's in production," the woman said. Then she threw her arms over her head and sighed loudly. "God you're a fucking miracle worker." Her breasts stayed high.

I suddenly recognized the client. She was an actress who'd starred in a famous teen sex comedy a few years earlier. We'd crossed paths at a few auditions before she hit the jackpot. I hoped she wouldn't remember me.

Meanwhile, Thad had spotted me and flitted over. He was lighter than a party balloon. He was the type of guy who led with his tummy. It paraded out in front of him like a royal vizier.

"Look at the trash blowing around these parts," he said.

"You come on pretty strong," I replied.

"Like a champagne hangover, sweetheart."

"I'm guessing that you're Thad."

"And I'm guessing you were class valedictorian." He offered me a soft hand. Already he'd plummeted to the bottom of my desert island list.

The actress had slipped on her warm-up jacket and sidled over. "This one is a total liar," she said to me, jerking a thumb towards the trainer.

"Oh, he doesn't care," said Thad. "He's just here to—" He paused so theatrically I could almost see the question mark pop over his head. "Why *are* you here again?"

"We had an appointment," I reminded.

The actress had cocked her head and was noticing me. That was okay. She'd probably tune out after a few seconds. Her type usually did.

But she stayed tuned in. "I remember you," she said. "You're—you're—" She snapped her fingers. "What's your name? We've met before."

"He's Frankie Fanta," said Thad.

She snapped her fingers. "No, I've met him at auditions."

I was about to join in the third-person fun when her cell phone went off and the actress took the usual steps. Phone to the ear, a swivel of the foot, and her voice receded to a mere squawk in the hallway.

The door clicked shut behind her. Thad turned to me. "Oh thank God," he said. "She smelled like giraffe piss. I swear, celebrities think they have a holy stink." He noticed me again. "So that little crudsucker Sam recommended me."

"He said you could give me some information."

The trainer's eyebrow went up theatrically. "*Por qua?*"

"April Kim."

He jaw dropped open, and for a moment he looked like a carp that had been surprised while trolling the ocean floor for trash. Then he lowered himself to the floor, cross-legged.

I squatted next to him on a rubberized aerobics step. "Do you remember her?"

"April *Kim.*" He spat out her name like a bitter cherry pit. "How do you know that girl?"

"I work for her," I said.

"Oh God," he said, clutching his face. "Oh God, oh God, oh *God.*"

"She takes some getting used to."

But Thad didn't hear a word. He was up now, circling the floor, frantically waving his hands at his face to cool himself down. "It's all coming back—"

I gave up on the exposition and sat back and inspected

my hands. They needed some lotion. I could admit that to myself here. Thad would understand too, whenever he was finished spazzing out.

By now the personal trainer was laying flat on the floor, arms and legs flung out wide, his chest heaving up and down. I saluted his performance.

"And the Oscar goes to you," I said.

He replied very slowly. "April Kim was the worst thing that ever happened to me."

TWENTY-EIGHT

"Tell me about it," I said.

The personal trainer jack-knifed up to a sitting position. It was a flamboyant display of his core abdominal strength. "You know, I'm not being fair," he said. "She was more than that. Look at this studio. Do you like it?"

That was random. "It does the trick."

"I paid for it with Kim money."

I nodded. "So how did she find you?"

Thad shrugged. "I still don't know. I just remember getting a voicemail from some weird Asian woman. You've been to their house?"

I nodded.

"Isn't it stupendous? I've been to wealthy men's houses all over Los Angeles"—he rolled his eyes in remembered pain—"but the Kims are beyond *fabu*."

"So what did you train her for?"

"I helped that little bitch become captain of her varsity soccer team. Now she won't return my calls." He swished his hand in the air. He was totally slappable.

"I bet she trained hard."

His eyes grew wary and guarded. "Have you ever seen a repetitive motion injury in a teenager?"

"No."

"It's rarer than a straight at Fire Island. At that age, the human body is too elastic. But April managed to destroy her left knee at age fourteen. I told her to slow down with the practice. No good. She was like one of those rats with the cocaine." He imitated someone making a series of fast kicks. "God, she's a nut."

We both sat there for a few seconds, listening to the muted rush of traffic below the window. Finally, with great effort, he tried to flip the conversation towards me.

"So what sort of slavery have they roped you into?"

"I'm supposed to help her get into Harvard."

He nodded, as if he'd suspected that much. "Did they ask you to move into their home yet?"

I started to laugh, but then saw his wounded face. He wasn't kidding.

"No," I said. "Did they ask you?"

Thad grew agitated, and I knew it was true.

"Did you accept?" I said.

He looked embarrassed, then exploded. "What? I'd *just* broken up with my boyfriend. It was free."

I shook my head. "I don't know. It seems inappropriate."

He fixed me dead in the eyes. "Usually this is understood, but I'll explain it since you seem a little simple. The Kims set the rules. There's no such thing as inappropriate—if it's what they want."

"Really."

"Of course *really*. And after I moved out, they thought it wasn't inappropriate to cheat me out of almost fifteen thousand dollars."

"Seriously?"

He nodded.

"So I'm guessing you filed a lawsuit."

He shook his head. "I would've been buried in legal fees. I knew it and they knew it." He looked very seriously at me. "Don't expose yourself to those people in any way. No home addresses, nothing."

"I understand."

He grabbed my wrist. "No, you don't understand. The Kims are wicked."

Something about the fear in his eyes made me suspect that he wasn't letting on to everything he'd seen.

I said goodbye and descended from the studio and back to my car. The engine was still acting up, but I managed to get her rolling and out onto the boulevard before sunset.

TWENTY-NINE

I drove up the road to the Kim mansion. By now, I knew every part of the drive. There was the speed bump, the curve, the short bridge spanning the arroyo, the seal on the mountainside to prevent mudslides.

But I'd changed. Thad had caused some of that. It's not every day that you're gripped at the wrist by a madman and warned to avoid a size-zero adolescent girl.

That's why, when her driveway rolled into sight, my heart started thumping.

April had abused me like a bastard stepchild, then flattered me like a Saudi ambassador. I felt paralyzed with uncertainty. I had no clue what kind of behavior would come next.

I parked the car in my customary spot on the street and pulled the handbrake. I'd never liked the long hidden driveway along the side of the mountain, the entrance that April had showed me. Staying on the public street made me feel better. It reminded me that I was only visiting.

I was buzzed through the wrought-iron gate. The gate shut behind me, the clang sounding heavier and more solid than usual. I followed the canopied tunnel of trees towards the house. The hairs on my arm stood up as the first chill of autumn fell upon my skin. I was grateful that there even was such a season in this edge-of-the-desert metropolis. In most years, summer just plowed straight into winter like a drunken kid with a stolen car into a telephone pole.

The Kim mansion squatted in the gardens, huge and fat and hidden, like a sumo wrestler. As I approached the front door, Mina opened it with a grotesque smile her face. Then she attempted to bow.

"Is April here?" I said.

The servant gave no indication of having understood. The smile just hung on her face. I decided that she had no soul. Peel away the mask and you would find another just like it.

The humpback led me down the hall as though I had never been in the home before. I watched her hump rise and fall with every step. There was something different, something off, about today.

We walked past April's study. The door was closed. I started scouting for escape strategies. She might lock me in a closet with the corpses of April's seven past tutors.

Instead, Mina led me to the father's library. I put on the game face as I entered.

Mister Kim was leaning against the desk with one ankle casually crossed over the other and hands plunged into his pockets. He was still dressed like a ninja in a black polo shirt, black pants, black slippers. The fine curves of his bicep could be traced under the banded sleeve of the shirt. His almond eyes betrayed nothing.

"Mister Jake tutor," he said, "where is your robe?"

He'd noticed. I'd forgotten to wear it today.

"I had a job interview," I lied, "so it had to stay home."

He stiffened at the mention of a job interview. Apparently he felt like he was my only employer. I noticed the sounds of a piano concerto emanating from a speaker embedded somewhere out of sight.

He lifted his hands and conducted lightly in the air. "I wanted to be a conductor," he said. "But the Korean National University of Arts reject me. Then my father break his back. I have to work." A surprised look spread across his face. "When he die, I feel so happy. I feel so *relieved*."

"It's hard to believe that," I said.

He regarded me with amusement. "You must come from good family. You must have money."

"Not really," I said. "I just try to see the best in people."

"Do you think other people are"—he grasped for the right word—"worthy of respect?"

"Yes," I said. "That's the benefit of living in civil society."

"Do you think about what is right and what is wrong?" he said.

"Not really."

"So you already know what is right."

I'd never thought of it that way before. In fact, I'd never thought I'd be having an exchange like this at all. I didn't know where in the hell it was going. He was holding the reins.

He poured a glass of soju and handed it to me. Then he turned back to the cabinet and touched a single fingertip to the woodwork. His eyes scanned the ceiling blankly. He seemed to have forgotten that I was there. I tasted the drink and waited for him to come back.

After a minute, I got tired of looking at his spine. "What is the point of this?" I said.

"Americans," he replied. "You always want to 'get to the business'. In Korea we drink all night before we get to the business."

He swung himself around and threw himself over the edge of a thick chair. One leg was flung over the chair's arm, like that of a slack king. "In a few weeks is the SAT," he said.

"Yes," I said.

"April is ready for the test?"

"Of course. But it's almost irrelevant for Harvard. They will be far more interested in her accomplishments."

"She is lazy."

"I don't agree."

"Oh, it's true," he assured me. "My daughter needs lots of supervision. But the problem is I have to go out of town for a few weeks."

"Where are you going?" I asked.

He betrayed nothing with his body. "China. And I need you to help her."

"Isn't that already my job?"

"No, I need you *all* the time." Jae Woo leaned forward in his seat. "I want you to live here."

THIRTY

Alarm bells began to ring in my head. They sounded a lot like Thad's voice.

"You want me to live in this house?" I said. "With April?"

"Yes," he said.

"For how long?"

He lifted his palms upwards. "She is senior, so she wants to have fun. So I say no, you must study, it's important. But she doesn't listen to me."

If only Jae Woo knew how April had locked herself in an upstairs bedroom to study during a raucous house party. Even if I told him, he wouldn't want to hear it.

Still, his worries were somewhat founded. Jarvis had briefed me earlier about how, in this supercharged admissions climate, universities were routinely rejecting students after accepting them. The logic: students who didn't care enough to keep up their grades in the last semester of high school weren't cut out for higher education. It was cruel, but the University of California, for example, that angry six-hundred-pound hippo of a university system, liked to throw its weight around by doing this regularly. Every June, one in forty future UC students receives a nasty surprise in the mailbox.

I tuned back in. April's dad was still talking. "But she doesn't listen to me. So we need you. You have to supervise her study. Help with her application. Make sure she come home on time. She listen to you, Mister Jake tutor. You graduate from Harvard."

He smirked a bit—as though he were proud to have hired such a prestigious person. I bit my lip and tried not to think about my second secret anymore. It was eating a hole in me. I had a feeling it wouldn't be much longer before somebody found out.

"So you don't trust her," I said.

"I don't trust anybody," he said, "especially not April. She always lie to me."

That itself sounded like a lie. She was manipulative and brazen, but I hadn't caught her in any open-faced lies, at least not yet.

"One question," I said.

"Yes, I will pay you," he said, already knowing.

"How much?"

"This much, each week." He wrote a figure on a piece of paper and handed it to me. My eyes grew wide. I'd never imagined making dough like that, not even in a month.

"It's a nice offer," I said, "especially to act as a glorified babysitter."

"She must get into Harvard," Jae Woo said.

A mad fire shone in his eye. I'd seen that same fire in his daughter too, and in the eyes of immigrants everywhere. It was a fire that had been lit in the old country, by ancestors denied education by imperial powers, by rigid class structures, by dreams deferred, by squatting on heels in rice paddies and sleeping on dirt floors.

"I don't know," I said.

"What is the problem? Is it not enough money?" He was miffed. I could see it from the way he shifted his weight. Actors like me recognize body language. His told me that, in his mind, I was already his property.

"I need to think about it."

"You don't need to think about it," he said, slightly exasperated.

"I do. Furthermore, I'd like to get some things in writing."

He cleared his throat. "Mister Jake tutor, I prefer we have trust. I don't like to leave too much paper."

"But you just said that you don't trust anybody."

He recovered quickly. "I trust *you*. With my daughter's future."

"Okay," I said, "this will be simple. Just sign a simple notarized document that you will agree to pay me this amount"—I lifted the scrap of paper—"for each week of employment."

Other people's faces would've writhed and twisted. But Jae Woo went icy cold instead. "I am busy man. You make that document, and I will sign it—maybe."

"Thank you," I said. "I will inform you of my decision."

"When?"

"Soon. Should I meet with April today?"

He waved his hand dismissively. "Not today. Go."

Without another word, he imperiously took the glass of soju back from my hand. Then he left the room in a huff.

I sauntered out of the house, back towards my car. I'd

stood up to a powerful man and negotiated my way out of a possible situation like Thad's. I felt like I'd just gotten up on my board and caught one of the biggest waves of my life.

Still, before I accepted his offer, I needed to talk to one more person.

THIRTY-ONE

To me, Italian food is a cliché. It's like the New York Yankees of cuisine—so successful, with so many big hitters, that eventually you find yourself exhausted, then finally rooting against it. I don't like to be on the side of Goliath.

That was one reason why I felt so uncomfortable at the bar of an Italian restaurant, the Mano, that night. A bartender with a face like a martini onion was rubbing steady circles into the countertop. His mannerisms—slow, deliberate, without a wasted movement—told me he'd been manning the bottles for years.

A moment ago he'd placed in front of me a glass of brown liquid that he'd called a *capo*. I'd felt older than him within seconds of sipping it.

The other reason for my nervousness was that I was waiting for my agent, Lew Sapelstein, to walk in the door. I'd called him fourteen times in the last two months. He'd ignored all my calls. Now I'd realized that the sound of my name had become as poisonous as an African toad.

It was sad, but it couldn't be avoided. In the entertainment industry, people hate relaying bad news. They'd rather leave a window open and let it be whooshed away silently on a breeze.

That was not my style. For me, there was only one remedy, and that was direct confrontation. It's probably the worst thing an actor can possibly do, but I didn't care enough about the business to talk myself out of it.

I put aside deep thoughts and swiveled around on my barstool. The Mano was packed full of young industry people wearing black Armani. They looked like seal pups. Their mouths made small talk but their shifty eyes darted around the room. It was my fault for coming here. I had about as much chance of a real conversation as I had of starring in a tentpole summer movie.

Besides the young guns, there were also the showbiz relics, the ones who'd survived the shakeouts, who'd somehow prospered, or who'd at least held on. I recognized a gray-skinned, saggy-paunched producer who was slumped in a corner booth. One hand running miserably through his hair, he was being visited by sad people like a deposed monarch. Then I remembered that he'd recently lost his deal at some studio to a younger up-n-comer with a single successful splatter flick.

Nearer to the center of the room stood a sweaty writer-director for whom I'd auditioned last year. It'd been a sidekick part in a single-camera comedy about two guys who move to Alaska to escape creditors. I didn't have the chops for it—funny is the most difficult and least rewarded style of acting. I'd known the audition was blown when the director quietly shook the leg of the camera during my reading. It was an old trick, a signal to fast-forward when reviewing the tapes later. That still irked me.

I scowled at him and turned back towards the bar. Then

I threw back another mouthful of old man liquor and felt my knees grow feeble.

Then there was a gust of air and a familiar voice behind me was loudly accusing the new valet of stealing his valuables. That's how I knew my agent had entered.

Lew Sapelstein was a regular here. A few years back, a loose-lipped assistant had shared this nugget after several tequila sunrises. I hadn't ever needed to use that knowledge until now.

I turned and saw the snarky ten-percenter slapping palms with the maître-d'. Between those palms, I knew there was a folded-up bill. He was that kind of guy.

An uncommonly light-haired child of Zion, Lew carried himself with the head-down, shambling gait of someone whose total lack of self-esteem carried him into places where he imagined he might find whatever part of his soul that he was missing. He could talk the ears off a deaf man because he was always trying to prove himself.

The cherry on top of this particular dark sundae was his rage. Lew used to erupt into quarter-hour-long tirades in which he would accuse you of everything from not washing your hands in the bathroom to undermining his power in the industry. The tirades had slowed down since he attended an anger management class. Since then, whenever the fever strikes, he stands over a recycling container and violently rips fistfuls of paper into tiny shreds.

When he greased past me on his way to a table, I saw my opportunity. "Hey Lew," I said loudly.

He swung his head up like a lantern on a chain. Not a glint of recognition in his eyes as they flicked from my face to my throat to my face. He said, "Hey there, guy. Long time no see."

Guy. Lew had forgotten my name; I was suddenly sure

of that too. "It's Jake," I said, sticking out my hand. "Jake Logan. I'm your client, remember?"

He snapped his fingers. "Sure, sure. Jake. You been working out? You look good."

"Do you think we can talk?"

"Aw," he said, "I got a date with this broad. I haven't been out with a girl for six months."

"Okay, Lew," I said casually, "some other time."

"You bet," he said. And then: "I'll call you."

There was a twinkle of gold, a pat on my shoulder, and he'd ducked into a corner booth where the maître d' was waiting with a pair of menus.

I turned back to the bar, depressed, and dove back into my wrinkle juice. The one chance to assert myself, my only promise to myself, and I'd reneged. I ordered two more *capos* and downed them in quick succession. The withered bartender was still rubbing his way to Shanghai through the countertop. That was all they probably let him do anymore.

Half an hour later, I allowed myself another quick glance at Lew's booth. An attractive twentysomething girl had joined him. She had chestnut hair and a nice face and large breasts, and Lew seemed to be trying his damnedest to concentrate on the first two items. It wasn't working.

Neither were his charms, judging from the way she was reared back in the booth like a wary horse, her upper lip pulling back to show her teeth. He kept trying to grab her hands. Her eyes kept glancing towards the door.

This was vintage Lew. I chuckled and turned to the bartender.

"Can I ask you a question?"

He fixed me with an empty stare that suggested a recent lobotomy.

"Does that guy meet many women here?"

The old man nodded once, slowly.

"Often?"

"A different one every night," he said. The voice sounded gargly and sick, like an old blender permanently stuck on low speed.

That didn't surprise me. A minute later, the girl approached the bar with her purse around her shoulder and her coat over her arm and asked for the bill. As the bartender stabbed at the buttons on the touch screen, I said, "I know that guy you were with."

"I wasn't with him," she replied.

"You had a drink together."

"It was a drink, not a marriage. I don't date perverts."

"No," I said, "he's not a pervert. He's just a creep. That's one step higher."

She rubbed her temples with her thumbs. "This place is so confusing."

I was soused enough to play smartass. "Naw, it's easy. There are walls, tables, glasses, plates, silverware. You order, you eat, you pay. It's pretty much the same everywhere."

"No, asshole," she said, "I mean the *industry*."

I made baboon lips and nodded sagely. "In that case, you're right."

She brought her forearm down strong upon the counter, as if cleaving it in half. "I can't ever tell what is *business* and what is *personal*. It's like there's no difference."

She looked up with the feverish eyes of a control freak who'd found herself in an uncontrollable environment. At that moment I knew she wouldn't last as an actress.

"Did he try to sign you?"

She nearly yelped. "That's what I was *hoping* for. Instead he tried to hold my hand."

"How sadistic."

She frowned. "I don't know why I'm still talking to you."

"Because you're a little traumatized and you don't have a girlfriend around right now."

She was eyeing me sharply now, the corner of her mouth crinkling up. "Who are you? An actor?"

I nodded. "Represented by your ex-boyfriend over there. But I'm a little jealous. He's never tried to hold my hand."

"I get the feeling he's a terrible agent."

"Give me your number and you could learn all about it."

I held her eyes for just the right amount of time—then broke the spell and sipped confidently from my drink. You have to measure out the indifference just right, a tablespoon at a time.

Honestly, I don't know why I asked for her number. Maybe I was a cat and maybe she was a piece of yarn. Maybe I was drunk.

As she wrote the bill of goods on a napkin, she gave me a weird smile, as though saluting my skills. I watched her walk out the door.

Then I fell off the barstool and vowed to find rubber-bottomed pants before I went drinking again.

It was time to confront my agent.

THIRTY-TWO

My agent was still sitting in the booth. He was holding his head in his hands.

I staggered over to Lew's table. "Hey."

"What do you want?" he said.

"She wasn't worth it anyways."

He looked at me through his fingers. "Leave me alone."

"You're supposed to at least remember my face, Lew. Faces are what get you paid."

He sighed. "Of course I remember you, Jake. I just don't want to *talk* to you."

I sat down opposite him and centered my drink on the table and looked him square in the eyes. "See, Lew, here's the problem. There's been a slight lull in my career. And I believe you're the one to blame."

Lew dropped his forehead onto the table. Then he slowly lifted his face and his gray eyes in their pouches fixed themselves somewhere past me.

"Do you want some advice?" he said.

"I'll roll it around my mouth and spit it out if it tastes bad."

He caught my eyes. "If there's even a single thing you like better than acting, go do it."

"Oh come on," I said.

"I mean it. This profession will tear your sweet little *goyim* heart in two." His face grew craggy and tough. "I've made good at least thirty actors like you. Nice kids. Fresh faces. Good skin." He reached over and dusted some invisible lint off my shoulder. It felt paternal.

"What happened to them?" I said.

"It's always the same. They get lucky, land a spot on a show that gets picked up for one, maybe two seasons. The wacky neighbor, the mouthy housekeeper, the slutty cousin —whatever. Two, three good years. Show ends, they go back to auditioning, can't stand it. Lost the fire in the belly. Eventually they slide out of the business. Leave the state and land a job teaching drama at some small college. Marry an old sweetheart, have kids, start jogging. Normal life. They know when to take their ball and go home."

He looked at me. The insinuation was clear.

"You're not putting me up for auditions anymore," I said.

He shrugged. "You got cold."

"Get me hot."

"It doesn't work like that."

"Make it."

He sighed. "You know what would be perfect? If you said that you don't want to be typecast either."

He was wrong about that. "I'd *love* to be typecast," I said.

Lew pointed a forefinger at my chest. "Damn *right* you would be. You should *be* so lucky." Then the anger passed and he grew reflective. "You had a decent run. You've got a good head on your shoulders. Plenty of things you'll do. What are you doing for money right now?"

I hated the way he presumed that my acting was done and gone, but I answered anyways. "Tutoring," I said.

He nodded sagely, as though he could see the grand strategy behind this decision. "With his grades, my kid'll graduate from auto mechanic trade school. He needs help. You want I should talk to him? Maybe you give me twenty percent off?"

"I'll give you something else," I said, and balled up the napkin with the girl's phone number and threw it at him. "That probably took you six months of begging. Me, five minutes."

He shrugged at my pitiful attempt at revenge. "You're young. You've got the quick game. Me, I've got three more lined up this weekend. It's a long game. One'll break eventually."

"Whoever she is, she'll call you daddy."

"I don't care. You're the short timer here. I'll still be working in this town in ten years."

That was a low blow. I walked away and paid my bill at the bar and left the old bartender a twenty-dollar tip for no reason whatsoever.

I'd already known that it was over with Lew. My contract with him was up in a month anyways. All I'd wanted was closure, which is the one thing you never get in the bizarre little ecosystem called the entertainment business.

And I didn't care much about the number on the napkin. That girl would quickly realize the idiocy of dating me.

After all, I was about to make the dumbest decision of my life

I went home and prepared to dive into the lake and swim into the weird lair to fight Beowulf's mother.

First I typed up a paper accepting the Kims' offer—and also spelling out the terms of the agreement. Then I went to bed early. The next morning, I took the document to a nearby notary public located in a narrow storefront on a nondescript portion of Wilshire. It had once been nothing and since then had improved to an afterthought.

The notary was a rotund man who was reading a boating magazine with intense interest. His pudgy fingers opened and closed into a fist seemingly on their own.

When I handed him the paper, he acted like he'd never seen such a request before in his life. He turned the document upside down, held it up to the light, squinted hard. Then he made a copy and read the copy very closely. Finally he whipped off his glasses and looked me up and down. He was going to try hard to find a reason not to stamp this.

"It's not authorizing the assassination of the president," I said.

"In this business, you never know," he said, then stamped it.

I paid him my fourteen dollars in cash and asked for a receipt. I sealed the agreement in an envelope and wrote April's father's name and address on it and peeled off a stamp for delivery. Then I dropped it into a mailbox. It would get there the next day.

I walked out into the sunshine and breathed in the fresh air. It was the first weekend of November. The weather was eighty-two degrees. It was days like this that had lured millions of people out of the dark and icy caverns of winters in other states. I remembered hearing that nearly half of Iowa had emptied into California in the nineteen-thirties.

With an entire day free, and a large guaranteed income not far off, I could've done anything. I could've gone to the movies. I could've slung a guitar over my shoulder and stuck a bottle of apple pucker under my arm and played at Robinson Crusoe at the beach all day. Or I could've gone the full Burroughs and shot heroin between my toes in a sleazy motel.

But my brain needs to stay busy, and I couldn't stop thinking about why nothing had been said, ever, about April's older sister, if she even existed. I'd only seen her in a single photo on the wall. And Jarvis had mentioned her at our first meeting. Beyond this, she was as mythical as a unicorn.

I pulled out my cell phone and dialed Jarvis. His weird secretary answered on the first ring and patched me through quickly.

"Just the person I was waiting to hear from," he said. His voice always sounded like it knew something you didn't.

"Buddy, I got a question for you."

"I've got a few too," he replied, "but you go first."

"I need a name."

"Whose?"

"April's sister."

He paused. "You're not thinking of contacting her, are you?"

"Maybe."

"Listen, your interest in April is purely academic. Don't go ripping off bandages."

"But she'll understand April," I said. "And I need all the help I can get."

Jarvis tried three or four times to respond to that one, but my reasoning was bulletproof.

"Fine," he said finally. "You want to find her? Here's what I know." I heard the sound of a file drawer being pulled open. "Her name is June Kim. She lives in the Kern Valley and works for the county. She's estranged from the family. All of that is confidential."

Two things shocked me. First, the Kims had named both their children after months of the year. Second, the oldest daughter of an overachieving Korean family had moved to an agricultural hinterland. The Kern Valley was one of the whitest, most reactionary counties in the state.

"Thanks," I said.

"You aren't planning to visit her?"

"Of course not."

"We encourage our tutors to go the extra mile. You're going about two hundred of them."

"How do you know these things?" I said. "You can't even see my sock."

"Because I know you."

"Okay, Jarvis. You win. The truth is that I'm becoming totally obsessed. This family is a mystery wrapped up in an enigma."

"Just take a rental in case she's still talking to her family," he said. "Give her a fake name. We don't want any problems. I'll reimburse expenses."

"Generous."

"Speaking of which, I have another present for her father," he said. "From a recent trip to Hong Kong."

"Why don't you just ship it?" I said.

"Because the Kims don't accept packages at their house."

"Paranoid."

"Definitely. Remember how much you don't know about these rich families."

That made sense. "I'll pick it up next week," I said.

"It's a long drive to the Kern Valley," he said.

I ended the call. It had been too easy. Jarvis had been quick to give me the information and even quicker to approve outside expenses. There was something weird going on. I sniffed the distinct odor of a hidden agenda.

THIRTY-FOUR

June Kim.

The name sat on my tongue like a pellet as I drove north out of Los Angeles. I said it to myself again. June Kim was a grandmother's name. It sounded like armchair doilies and floral mumus.

I pulled over at the top of the Tejon Pass and stared at the wall of blackened mountainside that surrounded the freeway. They'd been devastated in the recent fires.

Nowadays, Los Angeles spilled out almost fifty miles north from downtown proper. For the last half century, the developers had made sure of that. They just kept pushing it out, further and further, caught up in a race to build the biggest stucco box mansion. They pulled the curtain over the real costs, the wildfires, the astronomical air conditioning bills, the bad financing. Then, just as the new residents' poodles began to be devoured by coyotes, they stopped picking up their phones.

I slipped back into my rental car and coasted down the steep northern end of the pass. Northwards the entire San

Joaquin Valley, a hundred miles long, spread out in its green glory. This was the breadbasket of the state.

The air was already superheated by the time I hit the floor of the valley, and I turned off the freeway and followed a two-lane asphalt road that split the orange groves. I rolled my window down to let in the citrus-scented air. I watched the shiny green leaves and orange globules flash by. Los Angeles had looked like this once.

On the passenger seat rested a state map, and I consulted it at a stop sign. I was headed for Bakersfield, the county seat, to find June Kim at her job. I hadn't called in advance. This little jaunt was totally spontaneous.

I could only do this because I wasn't responsible for anybody but myself. I've never been married. I've barely had any girlfriends. Most women don't have a taste for my type of cocktail—equal parts instability and poverty, with a dash of bitter self-loathing.

Half an hour later I rolled into smoggy downtown Bakersfield. I found the county offices at the corner of an unremarkable intersection, across from a fast-food restaurant. It was housed in a weird box with a portico shaped like a wave. It screamed nineteen-fifties.

A sheen of sweat erupted on my forehead and my chest during the short walk from the car to the lobby.

I welcomed the blast of air conditioning. A receptionist was sitting behind a desk. She was a heavy old woman with a bulbous nose and a pair of sad bloodhound eyes. There was a romance novel in her hand. A slobbery hank of hair in her fingers told me that she probably had food issues. She didn't seem thrilled to see me.

"Hi," I said, "do you have a directory of county personnel?"

"You're lookin' at her," she said.

"That's quite a boast."

"You'd know everybody in this goddamn town too if you'd been settin' here for thirty-two years."

She tilted her head up sweetly and gave me a big smart-ass smile. It was her way of announcing that she felt undervalued.

"June Kim," I said.

"Never heard of her."

"She probably never heard of you either. Guess I'll leave now. Long drive back to LA."

The woman settled back and grinned. She loved this kind of snotty repartee. "Course I know her," she said. "I was just playin' with ya."

There was a pause while we both sized each other up. Her face had nothing whatsoever to do with her personality. Outside, sad sack. Inside—raging bull.

"How long should I stand here?" I said.

"Well, I kinda don't mind lookin' at ya. You been on TV?"

"No," I lied.

"But I seen you. I know it. Some kind of boxing show."

That made me almost lose my breakfast. This receptionist was the most observant viewer in the history of modern American television.

Four years ago, I'd had a couple days' work on a basic cable channel dramatic series about a boxer. I'd been a sparring partner to the main character, who'd gotten a little too excited during the shoot, and crushed the cartilage in my nose. I'd enjoyed about twenty seconds of screen time and forty days of recuperation.

"I don't think so," I said. "What about June?"

"Oh, she quit."

"Do you know where she went?"

"Sure do. What's it worth to you?"

"A big fat hug and a kiss," I said.

She was staring at me, offended. The scrim was quickly dropping on the scene. I sighed and played my ace card.

"You want the truth?" I said.

"That was you in the boxer show."

"Yeah."

"I knew it." She pounded the table with the palms of her hands until her cellulite shook. "What was Andrew Mauro like?"

Mauro had played the boxer. One hundred and sixty pounds of solid muscle—and gayer than peach cobbler in August. "Oh, he was just *fabulous*," I said. "Like pigeons and cherubs and gold rococo scrollwork."

"Yeah, I figured that out already," she said. "He couldn't take a hit. But you took 'em real nice."

"Thank you," I said.

"June Kim used to work here," she said. "But she didn't quit. She got fired."

"For what?"

"That's all you'll get out of me. I ain't losin' my retirement."

"Especially with it so many years away still."

She narrowed an eye. "You tryin' to get somewhere?"

"Depends on what somewhere looks like."

"It ain't seen any tourists in a while. Not your age."

She was pretending to despise our little exchange, but I was probably the most exciting thing to happen to her in months, her being chained to a desk in a building out here in this nowhere valley.

"You wear shoes?" I said.

"Not if I can help it. I got edema like you wouldn't believe."

"Then I'm gonna slip into yours for a moment," I replied, "and see if I can find out where June Kim might be found."

"Your tootsies are too small," she said. "But you entertained me, so I'll just tell ya. She's at a preschool down by the feedlot on Composa Boulevard."

"Really?"

"Yeah, she said it was too competitive here. Why you looking for her?"

June Kim had found a county job too competitive—a position for which there was no competition. I was starting to get a sense of this sister.

I dropped a couple of coins into the woman's cup and turned around. "That's for not asking."

"And that's my juice mug, you asshole," she said.

"Keep it," I said, "unless you want to find me to return it."

"I got your car on the security," she said. "Maybe I'll trace your plates."

"Bet you won't," I said.

I left the lobby thinking about how Jarvis' advice had helped in ways he couldn't have predicted.

THIRTY-FIVE

I stopped for a quick lunch at a taco truck and stood around swallowing my food alongside a group of *campesinos* who stared at me from underneath their two-foot-wide farmhand hats with the straps under the chin. Then I got back in my car and drove on further.

I found the preschool a few miles further on the ragged edge of a field of broccoli. I parked the car on the slanted shoulder, so it was tilted partway into the culvert on the side of the road.

The school was a square building with long eaves that shaded the four-year-olds who were arranged in a single file line along its yellow stucco walls. The front yard was full of monkey bars and hopscotch squares.

June Kim was easy to spot. She was the young Asian woman monitoring the lineup with ferocious control. She had a boy's short haircut, an athlete's thick legs, and a disciplinarian's intensity of purpose. She was like April without all the rainbows and lollipops.

A light breeze was blowing as I went through the front gate. I let it clang shut behind me, just to get her attention.

She didn't hear it. I stuck my tongue into my cheek and thought hard. A direct approach probably wouldn't work with her. It'd be better if she discovered me.

I squeezed my hips into a rubber tire swing to wait. I spun in lazy circles, stared at the sun. A couple of the kids were waving at me, but I didn't wave back. I was starting to feel a little creepy, a grown man loitering in a tire swing on a children's playground. But you can't spend your life worrying about what other people think of you.

Then June blew a coach's whistle, and the line of children started toddling inside. She stood near the door directing the traffic. After the last child had entered the building, she closed the door and switched to trash pickup. She swiped a candy wrapper from the grass. Her head scanned left to right as she patrolled the playground.

Then she spotted me.

She charged at me like a hippo mother protecting its young. "You can't sit here. This is private property."

"I'm looking for somebody," I replied.

"We have a front door. Don't sit there peeping on an entire class of children like an idiot."

She looked like she was about to seize me by the ear and haul me out behind the woodshed. I saw the resemblance to April.

"I'm actually looking for an adult," I said. "Do you know where I can find June Kim?"

That stopped her charge like a rifle shot. She even dropped back a little. It's always fun to play dumb.

She had the same idea of fun. "Why are you looking for June Kim?"

"Does she work here?"

"I need to know who you are first."

"Frankie Fanta."

She raised a puzzled eyebrow. "What kind of name is that?"

"My mom liked shitty soda," I said.

"That doesn't make sense," she said. "Fanta is your last name."

"You're a bright one," I said. "What are you doing working at a preschool?"

It was a legitimate question. I really wanted to know. But a dark storm swept across her eyes. "That's not your business."

I kept up the dumb act. "Okay. So I'm up from LA for the day. If you see June, let her know that I need to ask her a few things about her sister."

At the mention of her sister, June had gone stiffer than an ice sculpture. I could've whacked her with a hammer and shattered her into a thousand pieces.

"Why don't you leave your number and I'll give it to her," she said coldly.

I scrawled it on a napkin in my pocket from lunch. "Here. Tell June I'll be waiting until six pm."

I held out the number. Her eyes flicked from the napkin to my face and back. Then she crept forward and snatched it quickly.

I watched her go inside the school and shut the door. Then a curtain in a window parted and a pair of eyes watched me.

The sun shone down for a minute more before I realized that I was stuck in the tire swing. I decided to make the best of it and went to sleep. It was my day off.

Five minutes later my phone was buzzing in my pocket. I kicked and contorted and sent the tire spinning in wild circles before I could haul it out.

The caller ID read June Kim—as expected. I answered

it. "You can't sleep there," the voice said. "This is private property."

It was her voice. I saw the same eyes staring at me from the window. "Look," I said, "let's stop playing this game."

"No," she said.

"How many Korean women like you live in Bakersfield?"

"So you want to talk about my sister," she said.

"Yeah."

"I'll talk, but not here. See the barn to your left?"

I turned my head. Across the field of broccoli stood a long, shiny, corrugated-metal shed. A silo hovered behind it.

"Yeah."

"Meet me there in thirty minutes, after the school day ends."

"Okay."

"Oh, Frankie," she said, "walk there. Don't drive. It'll scare the animals."

She hung up. I spun uselessly in my rubber prison. My phone buzzed again and I answered.

"You have to get out of the swing," she said.

"I can't," I said.

"Try," she said, "or I'll send a class of toddlers outside to help you."

That got me going. It was a better abdominal exercise than any ball or piece of equipment. With outrageous effort I finally I planted both feet onto the ground, stood up, bent over, and pushed the tire off my butt.

There was the sound of little kids cheering. I saw them lined up in a nearby window.

THIRTY-SIX

I found myself hiking down the dirt road past my car, my hands plunged in my pockets and my nose crinkling at the air. It was heavy with the fetid smell of feedlot.

At the entrance to the barn, a sign read White Hills Dairy. Beyond was an extremely long row of black-and-white cows poking their heads through a fence. There was probably a quarter mile of them, lining the entire length of the road.

It was silent except for my footsteps as I began to walk past the lineup. The dumb broad bovine faces watched me. I felt the irrational guilt of someone walking past a row of prisoners. Then I reminded myself that they were outrageously stupid. You could punch them between their eyes and be in the next county before anything even registered in their pudding of a brain.

Soon the gamey odor grew overpowering, and I hiked my shirt over my nose.

Then seven hundred head of cattle later, I had arrived at the barn. There was a large silhouette of a heifer on the outside wall, and a red sign on the door reminding me that only authorized personnel were allowed beyond that point.

I was pondering the wisdom of sneaking in when the door slid open, and a stocky Mexican character popped out. He had a red neckerchief and elbows bowed out like the handles of a teacup. A cloud of shitstink billowed out behind him. It was so pungent that my eyes started watering.

"New vet?" he said.

Between coughs, I said, "Jesus, no."

"Who you want to see?"

"She'll be here in a minute."

"Who's that?"

"June Kim. From the preschool next door."

Those were the magic words. He nodded, then jerked his thumb behind him. "You can come in and flirt with the ladies, if you want. There's three thousand who haven't seen a man in a long time."

"No thanks," I said. "I don't like their perfume."

"But the girls just had their baths."

"I'll stay out here."

"All right." He pulled the sliding door shut and walked around the corner of the barn and disappeared.

I was left alone with my thoughts and a sneaking suspicion that this mission was an enormous practical joke. I even questioned my own judgment. Spending a day off traipsing around the blasted heart of the Central Valley wasn't really something a normal person would do. But I haven't been normal for years. I've been an actor.

A cloud of dust announced the arrival of another car at the main road. I watched it turn into the entrance and tear past the cows. They didn't seem too bothered.

It rolled to a stop next to me, and the engine cut off.

June Kim emerged wearing a pair of sunglasses. She wore them self-consciously. She didn't really belong out here in Kern County, and she knew it.

"Why'd you tell me to walk?" I said.

"To see if you'd do it."

I'd heard the exact same command from her sister. Already I felt the same distaste in my mouth.

"And if I hadn't?"

"I wouldn't have come over."

She stood insouciantly, looking at me with a hand on her hip. Neither of us said anything. It occurred to me that I needed to power this meeting.

"You probably want to know how I know your sister," I said.

She tipped her chin in the air but said nothing. She was five feet of drama in heels.

"My real name is Jake Logan, and I'm April's tutor. I've been assigned to get her into Harvard."

She didn't say anything, but I could see her tongue working itself inside her cheek.

"So I suppose April has been talking about me," she said.

"No, she hasn't said anything. She doesn't even know I'm here."

"I knew it," she said. "Those people don't let her say my name."

Those people. That alone spoke volumes.

"So you aren't on the best of terms with your parents," I said.

She laughed. "Dad expected me to go to Harvard. I didn't get in. Went to Stanford instead."

"He won't speak to you because you went to Stanford?"

"He's so old school about education. He bullied me

every day." She imitated him by lowering her voice. "'*Why you not get into Harvard? You not good enough.*' Telling people what a disappointment I was. How I was shaming him in the Korean community. It's all bullshit."

She sat down on the curb and picked a weed from a crack and violently ripped it into little pieces.

"How did it end?" I said.

"Two years ago. March seventeenth. At five in the evening." Her face tightened. "I stood up to him."

"What did you say?"

"I told him that he was pushy and obnoxious and that he should love me for who I was, not for who he wanted me to be."

"What did he do?"

A stony look hardened upon her face. "He disowned me."

THIRTY-SEVEN

There wasn't anything to say to that. When people reveal sensitive personal stuff, it's better to either say something noncommittal, or just shut up. I chose the latter.

"He changed the phone number," she said. "And the locks on the door. I had to pay for my last year of college myself."

"Stanford isn't cheap either."

"No, it's not." She looked at me. "So now they've got you to help my sister. Let me guess. You're an SAT guy."

"A little. Mostly it's because I went to Harvard."

"Oh God. I bet they worship you." She lowered her head between her knees. She was licking her emotional wounds. I've spent enough time around actors to know.

"Can I ask how you came out here?" I said. "In Bakersfield?"

"I didn't want to be in Los Angeles. I needed to escape." Her thought trailed off.

"To some place freer?" I said.

"To some place ... uncompetitive." She smacked the palm of a hand with a fist, like she'd just discovered something important. "Just helping people instead of stepping on their backs. Some place where people don't lie or cheat."

"So you found this job at a preschool," I said.

She nodded. "I tell all the kids to share their toys, to be nice to each other. I don't tell them that in a few years they won't be encouraged to share their things anymore." She looked wistful. "When does that happen, exactly?"

"I don't know."

She looked distant. "I just want to find a place where the people are good to each other. No gossiping, no lying, no exploiting. Just good people." She looked up like she had just remembered something. "So how's my sister?"

"She's becoming everything you hate."

An ugly look passed over her face. "I knew it would happen. She's got to get out of there."

"She has to *want* to get out of there," I said.

"They'll never let her leave," June said, "not after losing me. That house has a tractor beam. It pulls people in and destroys them."

I decided not to mention that I was sleeping in her old bedroom. "So what gives you clearance at this dairy farm?"

She stood up, rejuvenated and relieved to not be speaking about her family any more. "I take care of all their kids. You want to go inside?"

"It smells."

"Oh, just cover your nose. I want to show you something."

She trusted me now, because I'd listened to her talk about her traumatic family. I'd played this role before. Damaged people who are just coming to grips with their damage can't stop talking about it. They're the unlicked cubs. The entertainment business had been crawling with them.

Had been. It was hard for me to use that verb tense.

I followed her into the barn. Inside, the brightly-lit room seemed to stretch on forever. A thin corridor led between two rows of stalls. It was so long that it narrowed to a pinpoint. Above each stall the high rear end of a cow appeared. A single tube ran from the udder up to a tank at the door.

"Look at that," I said through my shirt. My eyes were watering.

"It's all done by suction now," June said. "The cows don't even have a choice."

We walked down the row. I soon grew bored. June probably was too. A question kept swirling around inside my head—and suddenly it blurted from my mouth.

"June, I've been dying to ask you something."

"Okay."

"What does your father do for a living?" I said.

"Did you ask him?"

"I did."

"What did he say?"

"Import export."

She nodded. "He always says that."

"It's not true?"

"It's true," she said. "Sort of."

There are many skills I don't have—such as gymnastics, knitting, calculus—but I do have intuition. I can always read people. And my intuition was telling me that there was a rich story to be mined here.

June leaned over the edge of a stall and rubbed the rump of a cow. "These poor creatures. Shipped around, no place to call home, nobody even knows they're alive. Somebody's getting rich off them, though."

I watched her closely. Her mind was somewhere else. Present but absent.

Suddenly she turned to me. "I'm ready to go."

I nodded. We turned around and went back the other way, between the rows of cows, and out of the barn.

THIRTY-EIGHT

When we left the barn, my compassion for animals was spent. I felt like having some steak and suggested it to June for dinner. She agreed to meet me, partly out of obligation, partly out of boredom.

I spent the afternoon wandering through downtown Bakersfield. It wasn't a good afternoon. The heat and the air pollution had me wheezing in less than an hour, so I ducked into a Mexican restaurant for a margarita. I drummed my fingers on the laminated menu while watching a soccer game on the television.

Later, we convened at another Mexican place, this one in a strip mall. There really isn't much else in Bakersfield. Under the harsh florescent lighting, the waitress brought red plastic baskets of fresh tortillas wrapped in aluminum foil, then a platter of soft flabs of *carne asada*.

Something had happened that afternoon to June. Discretion had gotten the better of her. Whenever I brought up her father, the clamp would come down, and she would change the subject. Same with the subject of her sister, except that she'd been temperamental, devious, and manipulative from a very young age.

The dinner came to a merciful end, and we said goodnight in the parking lot. I promised to call with news about her family. She gave me a half-hearted shrug in response. I realized that she was busy trying to divest herself.

I slipped into the rental car and began the drive back over the Grapevine. My mind was filled with speculation about the Kim family. An hour later, the lights of the San Fernando Valley came into view over the front of my hood. That's when my phone buzzed.

It was Jae Woo. I picked up quickly.

"Mister Jake tutor," he said, "I will accept your terms."

So he'd received the document. "Great," I said.

"You start tomorrow. You pick up April from her school. We have bed and meals. Mina will respect you and will accept your commands."

"Thank you."

"Mister Jake tutor, this is a big responsibility. I am trust you."

He ended the call. I felt my stomach doing flips on the rest of the way home. I climbed the narrow steps to my apartment and unlocked the rusty door and looked around. It was a small apartment, but it was mine, as long as I made the rent each month.

Tomorrow, however, I was losing that control. I would be living in a much larger home, true—but it wouldn't be mine.

I stared at the ceiling that night until the gray dawn broke over the sliver of ocean that was visible through the window from my pillow. It was the first time in my life I've ever had trouble sleeping.

THIRTY-NINE

The next afternoon, I sat parked outside Chandler-Beacon. In the backseat was a large softshell duffle that I'd packed. In my left hand was a grilled ham-and-cheese sandwich.

I chewed slowly and watched the exits. I was one pair of binoculars short of a stakeout. At first a couple of ragged kids came shuffling out, twiddling on their expensive phones. A few more followed, and soon the trickle became a torrent, all in a different mood—ecstatic, despondent, hyper-active, exhausted, pissed off.

I'd texted April to watch for me. Despite the odds, I quickly spotted her. She was dressed plainly in a red t-shirt, rolled-up blue jeans, and a tan pair of Uggs. The soft Australian boots made of fake suede had attached them-selves, like the jaws of an attack dog, onto the feet of local girls for the last several years. They showed no sign of letting go, either.

When April saw my car idling, she turned in a different direction. I cursed under my breath. She was going to make this hard.

I started my engine and followed her slowly as she walked across the parking lot. I kept one hand on my steering wheel and rolled my window down. "Hey, this isn't a coincidence," I said.

"What isn't?"

"I'm your ride."

She pretended not to hear me, so I jabbed the heel of my hand into the horn. It gave a quick, sudden, obnoxious blast right into her backside. She jerked as though she'd been zapped by a pair of jumper cables.

"Will you leave me alone?" she said.

"But I've got some candy for you, little girl."

"Stop being a creep. Where's Mina?"

"Having her hump polished. And you'd better get used to this creep because he's going to be living down the hall from you."

She turned around, astonished.

"Didn't your daddy tell you?" I said. "I'm your new nanny."

April immediately whipped out her phone and dialed a number, then hung up. "He must be in the air. Shit. I had *plans* for next weekend."

"Maybe you can still *have* them. You can tell me on the way." I leaned over and popped open the passenger door.

She reluctantly came around and slid herself into the seat with hateful resignation. I took pleasure in her torture.

We drove around the winding roads in utter silence. Then she crossed her arms and said, "How long are you going to stay?"

"It's open-ended."

She twisted around and saw the duffle in the backseat. "That won't last you more than a week."

"I can go home," I said.

"My dad didn't like it when the others tried to go home," she said.

I thought of Thad and didn't say anything. "So about the test," I said.

She writhed in her seat and clutched her hands over her ears. "God, who cares? Harvard barely even *looks* at this stupid test anyways."

That was debatable, but I let it slide. "They do care about this test, and your grades. I'm going to make sure that you keep everything high."

"How fun."

"You know," I said, "life is better when you mean what you say."

I didn't mean for it to sound like a lecture, but the way she looked at me made me realize that it had.

As I turned off Sunset and gunned the car uphill, I felt the power steering conk out.

"Goddammit," I said.

"What's wrong?"

"The electrical system. It just died."

This had been a long time coming. In my hands was suddenly a ring of rubber connected to a long shaft that felt like it'd been poured into wet, sludgy cement.

"Can you get us home?"

"I'll try."

I leaned into the wheel with every curve. It seemed impossible that people had ever driven like this. Maybe my car knew better than I did. Maybe it was trying to protect me from the Kim mansion—and the horrors within.

April was watching me struggle. A derisive smile lay at the corners of her mouth. I realized that she didn't feel people's pain. She merely mocked it.

At the family's hidden driveway, she hopped out and

laid her finger on the biometric sensor again. As we wound up the side of the mountain, the antique gas lamps felt more baroque, the jack pines more sinister. Everything grew darker. This was the heart of darkness.

I rolled to a halt in the same hidden visitors' space in the same vale, and as the engine died away, I suddenly knew that it wouldn't be starting again. I turned the ignition key to find out. Sure enough, it wouldn't turn over.

I slung the duffle bag over my shoulder and stepped outside.

"My car just totally died," I announced.

"It was a mercy killing," she said.

"I need to fix it."

"My dad can do that."

"Really?"

"He takes care of everybody inside the circle."

There was no doubt of that. I just wasn't sure that I wanted to be inside the circle at all.

I followed April towards the house. Even though it was bright sunshine overhead, the coolness of the distant November sun could be felt in the shadows of the trees, in the hidden mansion that lay waiting for me behind its curtain of ivy and foliage and darkness.

Mina opened the side kitchen door as we approached. She was wearing a chef's apron, which was splattered in liquid. Her mouth jabbered in Korean while her single squid eye fixed on me. She jabbed a metal cooking spoon in my direction. April answered her.

"What's she saying?" I said.

"We're discussing which bedroom you can take."

Mina had ripped the apron off her waist and snatched my bag from my hands. It was a grotesque parody of a bellhop.

"She also said that she'll call a tow truck," April said.

"Where is my car going?" I said.

She translated, and Mina answered briskly. "To our mechanic."

FORTY

I followed Mina down the main hallway. When we reached the foyer with the octagonal table, she turned and climbed the staircase. I presumed that I was supposed to follow, so I did.

Lining the walls of the upstairs landing was a series of gilt-framed photos of the family in earlier times. In every picture, Jae Woo was younger but still wore the same ninja outfit, and still possessed that same slit-eyed cunning look. I felt like he was staring at me from the past, daring me to intrude on his life.

June looked the same, only younger and fatter. April as a child, though, was a totally different character: light, happy, carefree. Her smile lit up every frame. I wondered what had happened to change that.

This level of the house was decorated in the same dark, seductive manner as the downstairs. Heavy carpeting, moody brass sconces. I spotted a couple more pieces of Asian statuary and guessed that Jarvis had sent them.

I followed her into a bedroom. It was completely white. There was a modest bed with a girly white headboard and a modest white bedspread. Sheer white walls, white carpeting, plain white chair. Everything felt shabby in a thrift-store way, as though it'd been well used.

Mina tossed my bag onto the floor and grunted, then motioned for me to follow her. In the hallway she pointed at a nearby door. Her mouth worked itself into an odd shape. I became aware that she was trying to form words.

"Va-frum," she finally said.

Bathroom.

"Yes," I said, "the bathroom."

"Binur ah sev-eh," she said. She tapped her watch.

Dinner at seven.

"Okay," I said. "Thank you."

The squid eye landed on me for a brief minute, and I felt a quick moment of appreciation pass between us. Then she swung that hump around and galumphed back down the hall.

I went and laid down on the bed with my arms over my head. It was a thin mattress, slightly depressed in the middle. It'd been well used. I stared at a painting on the wall. It was of a fluffy white dog with a red bow in its hair. The bit of red was the only spot of color in the entire room. I fell asleep like that.

When I awoke, the room had darkened. The stale air felt suffocating, and I fell off the bed and staggered across the room towards the window. My fingers scrabbled around looking for the seam. There was none. The window was sealed shut.

I stepped out of the room into the hallway. It was dark except for a pair of orange sconces on either wall. The carpet muffled my footsteps.

The bathroom floor was decorated with tiny black-and-white hexagonal tiles. It felt decades old. It was perfect for this place. The sink had a classic pair of handles and a deep basin. I turned on the tap and the water jetted out in a hard, clear stream. I splashed my face, rubbed my cheeks, and stared into the mirror. My cheeks looked hollow, my eyes looked nervous and bloodshot. I barely recognized myself.

I dried off on a white hand towel and went back to the bedroom to unpack. I found April sitting on my bed. My duffle bag was already opened and its contents had been dumped onto the bed.

She was holding up my cargo shorts. They'd cost me a hundred and ninety dollars at a painfully hip boutique on Robertson Boulevard.

"You're too old to wear these," she said.

"They're just shorts," I said.

She tossed them into a trash can. "It's a sign of childhood. Trust me, you need to dress older."

"Look," I said, "I am an actor. We dress young. And I *am* young. Not by your standards, but by everybody else's."

She found my toiletries bag and pulled out my mouthwash. "Are you an alcoholic? That's how my friend's mom smuggled stuff into rehab."

"You don't have any friends. Put that down."

She made a face and lifted out a small cylindrical black instrument. She switched it on. It made a buzzing sound.

She threw the object at me. "You're such a pervert."

"It's a nose hair trimmer," I said. "And going through my bag is way out of bounds."

"This is going to be so much fun," she sighed.

I needed to end this. "Two can play this game," I said. Then I turned to leave the room.

She sat up and looked alarmed. "Where are you going?"

"To rummage through your stuff. You know where to find me when you're done."

The ruse worked. She hadn't learned to get wise to head games. She followed me out the door and grabbed my arm.

"That's not cool."

"What's the matter?" I said. "Little girl doesn't like the taste of her own medicine?"

"I'm not a little girl," she said, jutting her jaw out. "I have the right to inspect the things you bring into my home. You may know us, but we don't really know you."

She did have a point, so I changed the subject. "So because I'm living here, we can work constantly, right?"

"When I'm ready for you," she said, "I'll let you know."

Thoughts of indentured servitude flitted through my head. I leaned against the doorframe. "I'm hungry."

"You slept through dinner. You can see if there are some leftovers."

I moseyed into the kitchen. Dirty plates, bowls, and cups were stacked along the countertop. It was as though somebody had been saving them up for several days.

Something soft hit me in the head and covered my vision. I pulled it off my face and saw that it was a white apron. I turned and saw Mina with a mean smile on her face. She pointed at the stacks. "*Wash-e*," she said.

"Me?"

She nodded.

"No," I said, tossing the apron back. "You *wash-e*."

Mina had anticipated that. She pulled a large combination lock from her pocket and waved it at me menacingly. She looked like a torturer waving around her electric clamps.

"Are you going to throw that at me?"

"*Wash-e*."

"No."

She walked over to the refrigerator—a custom-made,

industrial number—and locked the freezer and refrigerator handles together. Then she looked at my reaction.

"Are you serious?" I said.

She pointed at the stacks again. *"Wash-e."*

Then she waddled out of the kitchen with her hump rising and falling behind her.

I cursed her out for damn near forty-five minutes, as my hands were busy scrubbing and rinsing and drying. This wasn't anything close to tutoring. This was Mina lording over someone with lower status in the house. It was behavior of oppressed people.

When I was finished, I heard a click. Mina was behind me, unlocking the refrigerator. I found some barbecued beef, sweet potatoes, and an Asian pear inside.

I ate dinner but still felt somehow empty.

FORTY-ONE

I tried to sleep that night, but the long nap had beaten all the sleep out of me. Instead, I just lay on that flat bed inside that silent tomb, staring at the sworled ceiling tiles. There was nothing to listen to except the squirts of blood through my arteries.

At one o'clock am, I rose and put on a fresh t-shirt. Then I picked my cargo shorts out of the trash can and put those on too.

I slipped out of the bedroom and went into the hallway. It was darker than a blindfold. The smell of plums and hoisin sauce hung faintly in the air.

I didn't know where to go. I just felt restless. Down the hallway, April's bedroom door was closed tightly. She was probably murmuring vocabulary words in her sleep.

I headed the other way. I touched a light pad on the wall. Two rows of recessed circles in the ceiling cast cones of yellow light onto the sculptures lining either side of the hallway. It felt a lot like sneaking through a museum.

I went down the hall, treading quietly, and passed another closed door. April had said that this was Mina's room. She was probably even uglier when she was sleeping. I lifted up my fingers and hissed like a cat at her door. Then I kept moving.

Near the end of the hallway was another door, also closed. April hadn't mentioned anything about this one to me. I knocked quietly, just loud enough to wake up anyone inside who was sleeping.

But nobody replied. It felt like an empty room. I squeezed the doorknob between my fingers and gently turned it.

I knew right away that nobody was inside. It's funny how you can tell those sorts of things. The room was totally black. It was also colder than the rest of the house, which gave me the creeps. It had that dark energy of a room haunted with secrets.

I stood there shivering until the bright idea occurred to me to turn on the lights. The switch didn't do anything. So I moved into the room, arms straight out like Frankenstein, feeling around.

My toe hit a sofa. Where there's sofa, there's lamp. My hands finally found it, a chintzy number whose shade was made of some gauzy material. I groped underneath for the small knob, then turned it.

Muted light filled the room. There was an orange leather sofa. A modest television stood facing it. Across the room, a shelf held DVDs and cassette videotapes.

I was standing in a TV room. An entire room dedicated to the watching of filmed entertainment. It felt so freaking old-fashioned. But April's parents were like that.

I checked the television. The power button was missing. I'd bet my toothbrush that Jae Woo had gouged it out on purpose.

Then I wondered how many times April had really

been in here. People who played life at her level weren't comfortable with passive consumption.

Strolling across the carpet, I began to look through the Kim family's movie selection. It always kills me to see what other people watch. Not that it's so good, but because I usually know the backstory of each film production. Which actor was so drugged out that he had to be propped up by crew between takes. Which assistant director got sued by an extra for flinging a clipboard during a temper tantrum. This isn't the stuff you read in the tabloids or hear on the shows. A lot of it doesn't make it out of the industry.

The Kims' taste was weird. There were a lot of Korean horror movies. I knew that Korea was famous throughout Asia for its excellent cinema. I knew that because Lew had once set me up for an audition for the part of a tourist who gets clawed to death by an escaped predator rampaging through downtown Seoul. I'd lost the part.

There were other movies, too, mostly American teen comedies. That surprised me. I'd thought April was no less than forty years old in her soul.

Then I saw a cardboard box on the floor, under the shelf. It looked like it was trying to hide. I caught the edge and dragged it out and looked inside.

There were more DVDs and more videotapes. For a moment I was afraid that I'd stumbled onto somebody's pornography collection. But these were ordinary films.

The first movie I picked up was *Passing Lane*. It was a road trip comedy, two guys on the run from the law. It wasn't a good movie. I know because I was in it. I'd auditioned for the lead but was given the role of Short Order Cook #2, for which I'd had to learn how to flip a fried egg while muttering obscenities to the grill. It'd earned me fifteen seconds of screen time, plus my SAG card, so I couldn't say too many bad things about it.

I put that back and picked a different DVD from the box. This one was called *Demon Obsession*. It was about a young girl who is possessed by a demon and tries to seduce full-grown men. I was in that one too, playing a delivery man who gets dismembered on the porch by the swipe of a mysterious claw.

Two of my movies. In the same box.

That was a coincidence.

Then I put it back and shut my eyes and picked a third one. It was called *Boston Central*. This was one my first roles, an indie film shot for so little money that we couldn't even afford folding chairs on set. I remembered my feet being tired for the whole three-week shoot.

This had barreled way past coincidence now. This had gone over the cliff into obsession.

I got down on my knees and pawed through the box. Every movie here was something that I'd appeared in. Some of the videotapes were really rare, after-school movies, pilots for obscure cable channels that were cancelled after two episodes. A few had sticky notes on the covers, with times like 13:35 or 42:06 written on them. I recognized those times. They represented the exact moment when my part appeared.

I sat back on my heels. My people radar is good, and it hadn't noticed in April showing the slightest interest in my life. She was either a supremely good actor or ...

"What are you doing?" said a voice.

I whirled. It was April.

FORTY-TWO

April was wearing her pajamas, but not looking at all sleepy. She always stayed awake until three in the morning at least. A pencil behind her ear told me what she'd been doing. The usual.

"I'm playing a new game," I said. "It's called guess-the-stalker. Smart money is on you."

She looked down at the cardboard box. "Those aren't mine."

"Whose are they?"

She didn't say anything. I looked at her feet. She was hiding one foot behind the other.

"We can do this the easy way or the hard way."

"There's nothing to do *any* way," she said. "I don't know where that box came from."

"Then it's the hard way. I'll just assume you're lying." I rummaged through the videos again. "How did you find all of this? This is my entire archive. I mean, I don't even have some of these films."

April shifted her weight and looked uneasy.

I picked up an extremely obscure industrial video I'd

starred in. I'd spent two days walking casually around a chemical plant, describing OSHA regulations. "Jesus, April, this isn't even on YouTube. You must've done some real digging."

When the reply came, the voice was small: "Ebay. Someone else found it for me."

She looked extremely guilty. Part of her had probably wanted me to catch her. Girls were so crazy like that. "So you outsourced."

She shrugged. I was busting out laughing inside. April was so busy that she had farmed out the task of mounting a personal obsession to someone else.

"Just curious," I said. "Who got that job?"

She looked evasive. "A girl."

"What's her name?"

"Karundathi."

That was odd. Indian girls usually wouldn't play those games. Then it hit me.

I STARED AT HER. "You actually hired a person in India to scrounge up my entire back catalog?"

My incredulity must've shown on my face, because she grew instantly defensive. "What? It's like five dollars an hour. I use her for other stuff too." Not everything's about you, Jake."

I tried not to snort. April was trying to reframe the topic, but I didn't like being in someone else's portrait.

"You're unbelievable," I said.

"So are you. Can I give you some acting tips?"

This would be rich. Thespian advice from a walking cerebrum.

"Sure," I said, "as soon as you discover empathy, I'll take delivery of your critique."

She ignored me. I would have too. Instead, she went towards the box and pulled out *Passing Lane*. "The main character in this was totally unbelievable. His motivation wasn't clear at all."

"I didn't write it, moron. What about my performance?"

"You were trying too hard to seem mental. Try to internalize the characters more."

I had to admit that she was right. "Yeah, I had trouble thinking like a burger chef."

She reached down and picked up *Demon Obsession*. "Now, this was amateur hour, beginning to end."

"I was twenty years old."

"So what? You sucked. You looked like you didn't even want to be filmed that day."

She tossed it back, then picked up *Boston Central*. "Karundathi really liked this."

"And you?"

"It wasn't as odious as the others."

"High praise."

"That thing you did with your eyes in the scene in the park. It was good. Like Brando."

Christ, was she ever perceptive. "Yeah, I cribbed it from *On the Waterfront*."

She nodded. "If you're going to steal, steal from the best. Maybe this is a signpost for the future. Is it on your reel?"

I mumbled something, but she wouldn't let up.

"Who's your agent?"

Jesus. I clutched my head. I wasn't having this conversation with a sixteen-year-old girl. "Look, it doesn't matter. He's not calling me, is all that matters."

April had a cunning look on her face. "There's a girl Skylar in my class. Her dad runs one of the agencies. She's always talking about how she went out to dinner with some television star."

"So?"

"I can introduce you."

That was enough. I'd finished with this. It wasn't enough that the Kims had pulled me into the soft belly of their bizarre world. Now their tentacles were trying to reach into every nook and cranny of my own personal life.

"No," I said, "that won't be necessary." I took the DVD from her hand and put it back in the cardboard box. Then I shoved the entire box back beneath the shelf.

She was eyeing me oddly. "You look upset."

"You're a philosopher of the obvious."

"What's wrong?"

"Everything."

She was honestly upset. "Seriously, I want to know. Did I say something stupid?"

I rose to my feet. "Get out of my way."

FORTY-THREE

I moved past her, back out into the hallway. I went into my room and quickly began to throw all my belongings back into my duffel bag.

She appeared in my doorway. "Where are you going?"

"I've made a big mistake."

"Tell me."

"Sometimes we are reasonable animals. Sometimes we aren't. Coming here to live was one of my unreasonable moments."

"But I *need* you."

"That's a joke. You don't really need me."

"But I feel *lost* without you."

Now April was playing her best poor-me routine. I looked at her with barely concealed disgust. She was a five-foot-high piece of walking, talking, manipulative narcissism.

I zipped my bag. "You'd better get out of that doorway, or else you're going to get run over."

She didn't move. So I slung my bag over my shoulder and charged straight towards her. She squealed and ducked out of the way.

I went down the stairs to the main foyer. I could hear her footsteps pattering behind me.

"April, it's been a pleasure," I said. "Keep in touch—"

I put my hand on the door and tried to open it. It wouldn't budge. She was looking smug.

"Why is this locked?" I said.

"They always lock the doors at night."

"Who's they?"

"My dad."

"But this is locked from the outside."

She nodded. "They don't trust me."

"So when you come home, they're locked from the inside. When you're inside, they're locked from the outside."

April looked at me with sad eyes. She was fishing for pity. She deserved it too, but I wasn't giving her anything right now.

Instead, I stepped back and spun around, searching for another exit. "What if there's a fire? This isn't legal."

April shrugged. "Then we get toasted."

This was unacceptable. Thoughts of the Triangle Shirtwaist Factory fire raced through my mind, the women falling ten stories to the cement, their heavy black skirts ballooning up. But that's just my crazy trivial mind.

I headed for the kitchen. There was another door there. I'd come in that way after I'd dropped her off from the party, the night that I'd worn my bathrobe.

That door was locked too. I dropped my bag to the floor and mouthed a curse.

April had followed me into the kitchen. It was dark, except for her silhouette against the oven light.

"I'm nobody," I complained. "There's no reason to keep me here against my will."

"It's easier if you don't resist him," she urged. "It's easier just to give in."

Her voice was a purr. I noticed that her silhouette was getting closer. The hairs on the back of my neck stood up.

I was wearing a sleeveless t-shirt, and I felt her fingers running down the side of my arm. It was too late to change into a three-piece suit.

"Besides," she said, "even if you did escape, he'd find you. He can find anybody."

"Your dad seems like a powerful man," I agreed.

"Very powerful."

The unspoken hung between us like a cloud of noxious gas. Dark room. Horny teenage girl. Fingers on my arm. Powerful father.

There was no doubt about her intentions. April was dragging me into a minefield. I wasn't going there. Jake Logan had many options—options that were my own age, knew how to wear heels, could drink alcohol legally, and weren't paying me anything.

So I stepped backwards until my back was pressed against the door. She stepped forward. I could feel her stick-thin body press against the front of my own. It felt like being romanced by a grasshopper. I tried to imagine what it must be like to sleep with someone so tiny. I couldn't. My imagination failed me.

Her left hand curled around the back of my neck. It started to pull my head downwards. Towards her face.

"Kiss me," she said.

I found it suddenly hard to breath. My tongue moistened my lips. That was unfair. I hadn't asked it to do that.

"Kiss me *now*," she said. "I might not be in the mood again if you wait."

Jesus. She was demanding. I don't know why it surprised me. She probably scolded her shampoo bottle too.

My conscious mind was dead set against this, but I felt my body reacting in all the ways that male bodies usually react. This had to stop.

I placed my hands on her shoulders. It felt like gripping the handlebars of a tiny tricycle.

Then I pushed her backwards.

She stumbled backwards into the island kitchen. "What the hell was that?"

"You're sixteen."

Her shirt had hitched up. I could see her flat tummy. It probably would've turned on millions of other men. But sex wasn't what I was after.

"I turned seventeen last month," she said.

"Doesn't matter."

It still wasn't enough resistance, because she came back. Her hand clasped over mine. I could see what she was selling, and I didn't want it. That bottle of wine needed a few years to mature.

What I needed now were the principles of *jujitsu*.

"Okay, April," I said. "I can't resist."

My right hand snaked around her waist and pulled her close to me. I felt her breath suck in. Then my other hand crept down the side of her body into her pocket.

There it was. The small rectangular device was in the side of her sweatpants. I casually ran my fingers around its edges, just to be sure.

Then, quick as a snakebite, I yanked April's phone out of her shorts. My other hand planted itself on her sternum and pushed. She stumbled backwards. I was on the other side of the kitchen in a flash.

"What the—" she said, slow to react.

"I've got your phone," I said. "Now I'm going to find out who you've been texting during our sessions."

FORTY-FOUR

On my way up the stairs, I mentally patted myself on the back.

It'd been the neatest possible solution. Exiting an awkward sexual encounter by getting playful. Sure, it could be seen a step backwards for most guys, and maybe somebody less principled would've stripped her naked right there.

But those guys forget that teenage girls have five hundred different impulses in the course of a day. An offhand comment on an outfit, a change of music, a snub on a social networking site—all of it can change their entire worldview.

April was no exception. She could've gone to the police. She could've told her father. She could've turned into a stage-five clinger. It was impossible to predict. I would've lost my freedom, my reputation, and what little of my self-respect that remained.

Also, it would've been flat wrong.

Yes, this was the best way. Even if she were my own age,

the only interesting physical asset she had was her brain. She seemed about as sexy as a tray of forks.

By now April had recovered her senses and was chasing me up the stairs. Her face seemed alive. No woman likes to be sexually rejected and robbed at the same time.

"You can't take my phone," she said.

"And banks aren't supposed to gamble with people's pensions," I said. "Life's not fair."

Now she was bounding up the steps, two at a time. I looked back. Christ, she could move fast when she wanted to.

I hit the top of the steps, ran down the hall, and dove into the bathroom. I slammed the door shut and locked it behind me.

The sound of April's pounding fists echoed against the tiles. I could hear her shouting something, but I'd already tuned her out.

Her phone was businesslike, powerful, encased in simple black rubber. It could've belonged to a telecom executive with a forgettable face. I hit the power button. The word Locked appeared below a digital keypad.

Of course it would be locked. Now I had to guess her numerical code. Suddenly it came to me. This would be too easy.

I typed 1600 into the keypad. The perfect score on the SAT. It worked. The screen dissolved and resolved into a picture of April's scowling face.

"You are so predictable," I said.

An unearthly shriek slid under the doorframe. "Get *out* of there!" she was shouting. "That's *my phone!*"

I sat down on the toilet. This was delicious revenge. "Let's see who you've been texting first."

I found the sent messages folder and began to read.

Keep in mind, this isn't something I normally do. But April had shown me that there were no boundaries in our relationship. And honestly I hadn't been expecting much. Maybe some bullying reminders about assignments due. A couple of angry rebukes. Pretty much nothing positive.

My jaw dropped. They weren't at all like that. I learned that April had been agonizing over her brand of eyeliner for several months. I learned that she was considering having surgery to correct her bone spurs on her feet. I learned that there were three boys in her grade that were worth pursuing —and that she had a crush on none of them.

Then I saw this one:

omg my tutor is so hot i cant wait til he moves in

I stared at that one for a while. It wasn't news, really. She'd just tried to seduce me in the kitchen. But it was weird to see the crush written out, especially in such bad textspeak. After all, I'd read April's academic papers. Her syntax was perfect. She could practically be an editor.

She was throwing herself against the door now. "Oh my *God*, this is so *unfair*—"

"If you'd had an older brother," I said, "you could tolerate this type of harassment better."

I scrolled through the messages, looking at the recipients. Some of the names I didn't recognize. One was in Korean. But ninety percent of her communication—the girliest stuff—was to someone named Hannah.

Hannah. I hadn't heard her mention that name before.

An unusual sound outside the door caught my attention. It was the clink and scrape of metal on metal. I looked over. The doorknob was moving around.

April was using tools to break in. I powered her phone off, went over to the door, and unlocked it.

Mina was standing there with a power drill in her hand.

She had a t-shirt and long sweatpants. A nightmask had been pushed up on her forehead. Her hump rose from her back like a nightmare.

April stood behind her, hands on hips. I tossed her the phone, and she barely managed to catch it. "Thanks for letting me borrow that," I said.

Then I walked to my bedroom and shut the door.

FORTY-FIVE

She didn't bother following me after that, so I went straight to bed. But I still couldn't sleep.

A few minutes later, the distant sound of crying started. It sounded muffled. I lay there, listening to it for a while. It rose and fell, in pitch and in volume. It sounded like someone was crooning herself to sleep.

She couldn't sleep either. I waited for what felt like an eternity. When I looked at the bedside clock again, it read 3:00 am.

I rose from bed and went back out into the hallway. I walked down to her bedroom and knocked on the door.

"What?" she said.

"Can I come in?"

There was no answer. I'd upset girls before, and this was the closest I was going to get to a yes. So I pushed open the door.

April was curled in the corner of her bedroom, on the floor. There was nowhere else to sit. It was bed or carpet. The walls were bare. An open closet showed some clothing. This was a room for sleeping and dressing.

A single lamp on her nightstand cast a yellow glow upon her black hair. She was clutching a small teddy bear. She was stroking its head and singing to it.

I stood there in the doorway, feeling older than ever in our relationship, feeling guilty for no reason. I hadn't taken her virginity. But I had taken her privacy.

"What do you want?" she said.

"What's that little guy's name?"

"Churchill."

"How British."

She wiped the teddy bear's nose. She was fussing with it. "I was obsessed with Winston Churchill when we bought him."

"How old were you?"

"Seven. He goes everywhere important with me. He sleeps under my pillow."

I sat down on the carpet beside her. I made sure to face away from her, so that we were side by side. It was less threatening this way.

"So if there was a wildfire coming, and you had to evacuate your house," I said, "what would be the first—"

She answered before I had finished. "Churchill. For sure."

"Not Monkey?"

She shook her head. "Churchill is my favorite."

I nodded. Stuffed animals could be that important. I'd had a froggy blanket that'd meant the world to me, and I'd for longer than I'd like to admit.

Neither of us said anything for a while. It felt like we'd just been through a war. If either of us had smoked cigarettes, we probably would've shared one.

"Can I ask you something else?"

"Maybe."

"Who is Hannah?"

She sat up wearily. Her body language seemed to change. This seemed to be the very heart of whatever she was trying to protect.

"She's my friend."

"Does she go to your school? I've never heard you mention her."

"No, she doesn't go to school."

"Then what does she do?"

April sighed. "I met her while I was doing the teen internship at Cedars-Sinai Hospital last year. She's in the oncology ward."

That took a minute to sink in. "You mean she's sick?"

April nodded. "She has cancer."

"How's she doing?"

She made a fifty-fifty motion with her hand. "It's kind of month-to-month right now."

April had made friends with a sick girl. That was unexpected. Of course, you could look at it another way too. Maybe April was so socially incompatible that she had to prey on sick people for companionship.

Then she turned and looked at me. "So what did you learn about me when you were looking through my texts?"

She seemed vulnerable. I chose my words carefully. "That you're just a girl inside. A teenage girl with crazy emotions."

"Duh."

I turned my head. Now she was staring deeply into her teddy bear's eyes, as if she were looking into a happier place.

"Pardon me," I said, "but you *do* realize how absurdly far you go to show people just how mature you are."

"So what?"

She was defensive now, so I resumed eggshell duty. "It's really hard to be around you sometimes."

"I know I'm different. I don't fit in. That's why you didn't want to kiss me."

My heart dropped in my chest. This bizarre monster of a girl had the uncanny ability to pull my heartstrings. Still, it was time to draw some boundaries.

"I need to make something clear about our relationship," I said. "This is an academic one. Not a romantic one."

She buried her face in Churchill's belly. "I know I'm not attractive to you."

Jesus. I tried to find a way to make her feel better without losing my own dignity. "April, you just need to find someone who likes your particular type of attractiveness."

She gave me a dark look. That probably sounded worse than I'd meant it to.

"Whatever," she said. "You're, like, thirty years old anyways."

I bristled at that. Being an actor in Los Angeles had made me sensitive to my creeping age.

"No," I said, "you are way too young for *me*. And too skinny."

I shook her bony upper arm. She yanked it away, annoyed. "I'm trying to gain weight. It's not working." Then she straightened up. "Look, this is a stupid conversation anyways. I can get a *much* better guy than you."

"I'm sure you can," I lied.

"I just don't want to right now," she continued. "I'm way too busy."

"You're really busy," I agreed.

Her rationalization hamster was busy running on its wheel. That was fine. It gave me a great way out of the conversation.

I stuck out my hand. "Tutor?"

She paused, then shook it. "Student."

"Don't act so pained to say that."

She shrugged. I said good night, stood up, and went back to my room.

It felt good to see April's armor fall away. But it didn't change the fact that I was still trapped in this mansion.

FORTY-SIX

One week later, on a Friday morning, I was standing over April's chair, bouncing a paddleball near her ear. *Pock pock pock pock pock pock.*

I hadn't left the Kim mansion in a week. By April's request, I'd been feeding her endless SAT drills in preparation for her test date on Saturday. This was her last chance to take the test before college applications were due. The paddleball was the latest of my wicked schemes designed to destroy her concentration. She loved the challenge. Inside her tiny chest beat the heart of a sadist.

"Let's go, Kim," I shouted, then blew a coach's whistle.

Her brow was furrowed deeply. I could see her feverishly working out a math question. I peered over her shoulder. It was number twenty, the last one in the section, and typically the hardest. This question was an ugly mixture of ratios and probability. It was a real stomach churner. I'd spent ten minutes figuring it out in my room last night. April had only two minutes.

"Time's up," I finally said. "Lay down your pencil and prepare for community college."

She bubbled her final answer, sat back, and exhaled. "The paddleball is a new one. Where'd you get that?"

"I found it in your toy chest in the basement," I said.

"That was my sister's. I didn't have a toy chest."

"You can play in it later when you're staying home instead of going to college. Give me the answer sheet."

I took the answer sheet from her and sat down at the other table with my colored pencils and calculator. I started going up and down the lines of bubbles, marking the incorrect answers.

April came and stood over me. She was waiting for her results. "You seem to be doing well," I said.

"Is that the truth?"

"Yes. Go over there and leave me alone until I'm done."

Soon I'd finished the scoring. She'd missed two critical reading questions, one grammar question, and no math questions. I consulted the conversion chart. It was enough to give her a perfect score. Only two hundred and fifty students in entire world typically achieved that on any given test date.

This was extraordinary. I wrote 2400 at the top of the answer sheet and circled it twice. Then I quickly flipped it over.

I looked up sweetly at her.

"Let's talk about how to prepare for the real test tomorrow."

"What did I get?"

I waved the question off. "All in good time, princess. You have any plans tonight?"

"No."

"Good. Keep it that way. No studying, no reading, no working—no mental concentration of any kind. This is a monster of a test tomorrow. Eat a good breakfast with lots of protein. That means no white rice, you dumb Korean."

"Shut up."

"And also bring a couple of candy bars."

"But we're not allowed to bring food into the test."

"You can sneak them in the pockets of your coat. During the breaks, just go into the bathroom and shove them down your throat like a bulimic. Trust me, you'll need that energy."

She was smiling. "What else?"

"Change the batteries in your calculator."

"I already did it."

"Then you're all set."

"So now are you going to show me what I scored?"

I decided to tease her. I slid the paper towards her, lifting the edge ever-so-slightly.

"Is it good news or bad news?" she said.

"That depends on your perspective."

April's eyes lit up. "That means it's good."

She lunged for the paper. I yanked it away. It was a playful standoff. I stood up and raced around the table. She chased me. We were both letting off a lot of steam. It'd been a heavy week.

We fenced off around a chair. She dodged left, I dodged right.

"Give it to me," she said, giggling.

"Tell you what," I said. "Let me read your personal statement for your college applications first, and I will reveal the score."

"No."

"Come on. You know you should get other people's feedback."

Her face grew hard. "I don't *need* feedback."

"Then you won't find out the score."

April made a last-ditch lunge for me directly over the chair. I tucked backwards into a somersault and popped up easily out of her reach.

She was bent over, breathing heavily. "Fine." She went over to her laptop, opened it up, and opened a document. "I just finished it yesterday. Be nice."

"Why? You're not."

"Because it's personal to me."

"All right."

"You promise to be nice?"

"I promise."

She gestured to the podium. April was the only person I knew who used a laptop standing up, like a conductor. I folded the results of her test and slid them down my shirt.

"Tricky," she said.

"Of course." I went over and began reading. I'd finished it two minutes later. It was a phenomenal essay, heartfelt, original, funny, serious, non-clichéd. She'd walked the tightrope perfectly.

I was trying to figure out how to welcome her to Harvard in a witty way when something interrupted me. It was the sound of footsteps in the hallway. They were heavy and angry. It sounded a lot like Jae Woo. I'd managed to avoid the man for the better part of the week, despite the fact that I was a prisoner in his house.

A moment later, he swept into the room. He was wearing his customary black outfit. His eyes were two pools of darkness, inscrutable and unfeeling.

"Mister Jake tutor," he said.

"Jae Woo," I replied, "it's nice to see you."

But he hadn't stopped by for a social call. He poked a finger towards me. "I have something to say to you."

My stomach dropped. "What's that?"

"You are a liar."

FORTY-SEVEN

I felt my blood run cold. There was something about this man that unnerved me. He seemed cool on the outside, and something told me that, if you peeled back the layers of his onion, you would find a frozen center.

Even worse, I knew exactly what he was about to say. I'd been rehearsing this moment for weeks now, wondering when my past was going to catch up with me.

It was my second secret, the one I don't like to talk about—and he knew it.

"I called Harvard," he said, "looking for your records."

I couldn't meet his eyes.

"They say you not graduate. What happen?"

I tried to speak, but the words wouldn't come to me.

"Answer me."

"Okay," I said. "The truth is that I didn't graduate from Harvard. I got kicked out."

There it was, dragged out into the open. My second secret. Then I coughed, shuffled my feet, looked around stupidly.

He stood with his hands on his hips. "So you never go to Harvard?"

I held up a finger. "No, I went to Harvard for three years. That part is true."

Jae Woo just stood there, taking in the news. I could see his mental gears grinding. How much loss of face he would suffer in his community if it was revealed that his daughter's tutor did not, in fact, graduate from an Ivy League institution.

I knew this was coming too. I'd explained it to many, many people over the years. Casting directors, apartment landlords, bank officials, you name it. Word got around, and soon this reputation was one of the reasons I was hired for acting jobs. After all, getting booted from Harvard was a great story. It made me look like a bad boy or a genius, even though I'm neither.

A look of severe judgment hung on Jae Woo's face. "Why?"

I drew a deep breath and began to talk. The story behind the expulsion is much less glamorous. I haven't had as much practice telling it.

Here it is anyways.

AT HARVARD, I'd been friends with a kid named R.J. McClean. He was a sad kid with a mopey face who was good at the classics—a major, by the way, that is the secret back-door entrance into the Ivy League. Anyways, R.J. was poor. His family had taken out a second mortgage on their house to afford the tuition at Harvard. We had a lot in common.

In November of our senior year, his father had died of a

sudden heart attack. R.J. left school for three weeks. He came back on the Friday before finals week. The Harvard administration must've had an axe to grind against poor students with dead dads, because they decided to give him no extension on the finals. He'd already been in academic trouble, and if he didn't pass all his classes, he'd be expelled.

R.J. and I had shared one class—History of Modern Architecture, taught by an old man who had literally written our textbook. I had loved the class, but hated him, mostly because he'd never taken questions and he'd never kept office hours. He'd technically been my professor, but I probably could've saved the tuition money and just checked out his books from the library instead.

There had been no way R.J. was going to learn three weeks of missed slides in one weekend. He couldn't concentrate after the funeral. I'd watched him stare into space at lunchtime, forgetting about his food. He'd been slipping into a depression right before my very eyes.

So I told him he could copy off my test.

It wasn't my proudest moment, but it would keep him from flunking out. And it was a middle finger in the face of the Harvard administration, which was apparently too busy counting its thirty-billion-dollar endowment to care about the life of a piddly undergraduate.

During the final, we'd sat kitty-corner from one another in the darkened room. I'd executed all the classic cheater's moves, edging the paper closer to him, sinking my shoulder, two coughs for choice B, three for choice C. You know how it goes.

What I hadn't known was that the teacher's assistants had been standing in the aisle behind us, monitoring the room.

The end had come swiftly. In less than three days, I'd

been notified of the academic board's decision, packed up my room, and moved to my own apartment a few miles off campus.

I'd bounced around doing odd jobs and feeling sorry for myself for a few months. Then I'd landed my first acting gig in an indie movie. It was *Boston Central*, the movie I mentioned earlier, an indie drama about Boston ganglife, a young Irish kid trapped between wanting to stay in and get out. Not exactly a new idea, but I'd won a supporting role as a wisecracking bartender, after the executive producer had seen me slinging black-and-tans at a local pub.

My first day on a movie set was the day that I should've gone to my class graduation.

The movie won an Independent Spirit Award. I wasn't mentioned at all, but all the fuss did draw the attention of Lew, my reptilian agent. He's the one who told me to move to Los Angeles to join the rest of the emotional basketcases.

There you have it. My life.

I GAVE a shortened version of this story to Jae Woo.

"So they kicked you out for cheating," he finally said.

"No, they kicked me out for *helping* somebody else cheat," I replied. "Somebody who really needed it."

I could tell from the look in his eye that this wasn't going to fly. Fortunately, I had backup.

I reached into my shirt and produced April's folded up test summary. "Look at this."

He unfolded the paper. April ran around to his side. When she saw the number, she started squealing.

"Do you see?" I said, pointing to the score. "Twenty-four hundred. A perfect score."

He betrayed no emotion. "Every question right?"

I knew he was going to ask that. "No, she missed three questions, but there's a curve, so the colleges will never know. To them, it's a perfect score."

This pleased him. His reputation in the eyes of others trumped everything else.

"Now," I said, "we just have to make sure that she performs the same way on the real test tomorrow."

His black eyes looked at me. There was nothing behind them. "I hired you to do this."

"You did."

"I will call Mister Jarvis and tell him that we are finished."

That was my entire thanks. He handed the sheet back to me and left the room. I was unsure what had just happened. Was he going to tell Jarvis how pleased he was with my work with his daughter? Or how disgusted he was with my sin of omission? It was hard to tell.

I turned back to April. She was trying to dance. It looked like she was having a conniption fit. Joy wasn't a customary state for her.

She whirled around. A big smile was on her face. Her eyes were shining. "I *did* it."

"Not yet," I reminded her. "That was practice. You've got to sleep tonight, then take it for real tomorrow."

It didn't matter. She let out a squeal of excitement—then galloped across the study and threw herself onto me. Her arms hooked around my neck. It was a little girl's move, child-like, uninhibited.

I wasn't expecting it. Her velocity still knocked me backwards on my heels. But she maintained her insanely strong grip around my neck.

Too late I realized that I was going to lose my balance. I

staggered backwards. My upper back collided with something heavy and ceramic. I crashed to the floor like a sack of beans. I felt the object shatter between my shoulder blades.

April had fallen on top of me. "Oh my God," she said. "I thought you were stronger than that."

"You tackle someone without warning," I said, "that's what's going to happen."

The girl rolled off me. I sat up and looked back at the wreckage we'd caused. The ceramic object that had shattered was the terra cotta horse—the gift from Jarvis that I'd brought inside a gold gift-wrapped box weeks earlier.

April knelt down among the pieces. She began picking them up and depositing them into her trash can. "God, I hope this was just a replica."

"Me too."

"Can you get down here and help me clean this up?"

I knelt down next to her and began collecting the pieces. "Are you going to tell anybody?"

She shook her head. "Mina might notice, but I'll make sure she doesn't talk."

"Thanks." I really didn't want to be handed a bill for a smashed piece of East Asian artwork.

Then April stopped. Her fingers had picked up something small.

"Jake, what is this?"

In her hand was part of the broken horse's head. She was holding it out towards me. There was both fear and suspicion on her face. I looked more closely.

Attached to the inside of the head was a small microphone.

FORTY-EIGHT

The small bit of black plastic and carbon was no bigger than a thumbnail. It was attached to a small transmitter. There was a tiny LED light too. A green one.

That meant it was synced up—and recording.

"Is that a microphone?" she said.

"Probably, but I'm no expert."

Her hand began trembling. "Why is there a *microphone* inside a centuries-old terra cotta horse?"

There was no answer to that question, and I admitted as much. "I don't know."

"And why did *you* bring that thing into my family's house?"

Her eyes were roving all over my face, looking for a sign of deception or fraud. It wasn't there. I may have been clueless, but I wasn't lying.

"Because Jarvis asked me to."

She didn't respond.

"Maybe I should call Jarvis about this," I added. "Maybe he didn't know it was there."

"Maybe you shouldn't do anything." Her fingers were sweeping up the rest of the shards and dumping them unceremoniously in the trash. "I knew I shouldn't have trusted you."

I sunk my chin into my chest and exhaled sadly. "April, I swear on everything that is good and holy—I don't know what this goddamned microphone is doing inside this statue."

"How do I know you're not lying again?"

It had been a long struggle trying to put the issue of trust to bed. But this ludicrous accident, and this mysterious microphone, had resurrected the conflict.

I got to my feet and followed her across the study. She had her narrow back turned towards me. I laid my hand on her shoulder.

"Don't touch me," she said.

I removed the offending hand. "What can I do to make you trust me again?"

"I don't know."

Now the last of my patience had leaked away. I grabbed her shoulder and whirled her around.

"Hey—"

"Listen," I said, "I don't know what kind of business your dad is in. And guess what? I really don't care. I only have one purpose here."

"What's that?"

She was waiting for it, so I gave it to her. "I'm here to help *you*. That's it."

My finger poked her in the sternum to emphasize the point. She seemed to be chewing that over, so I fed her a little bit more cud. "I'm just a tutor. Nothing more."

"You're an actor," she reminded me.

"A failed one."

I could sense her coming back to my side. Her eyes were staring at something intensely. "Then what is Jarvis? He hired you, didn't he?"

That question had been pressing into my skull like a nail. "I don't know what Jarvis is, but I'd like to find out."

I pulled out my phone and dialed his number. I listened to the ringing. It seemed to last an eternity. April watched my face the whole time. It went to his voicemail, so I hung up.

"He didn't pick up."

Her tiny fist struck the palm of her hand. "I think he's been spying on my family."

That was entirely possible. I remembered all the other pieces of Asian art in the house. There could be a microphone, or a camera, in every one of them. Why a private college counselor would need to spy on a family was beyond me, though.

Suddenly I knew that leaving a voicemail wasn't going to do justice to the gravity of the situation. I had to talk to Jarvis in person.

"I need to go see him," I said.

"That's a good idea," she said. "I'll walk you out. You'll need my thumb to get out of the gate."

"That's locked from the outside too?"

"It shouldn't surprise you by now."

I sighed. "Your family lives like Russians. Everything is prohibited except that which is permitted."

"No," she corrected, "even the stuff that's permitted is prohibited. Follow me. Walk quietly."

I followed her out of the study and quietly down the hallway to the front door. She placed her fingers on the handle and squeezed. The door swung open. It didn't make a sound. I gave thanks for small miracles.

Outside, we moved quickly, past the rows of small piles of dirt that signaled the potted kimchi. I wondered how bad it would smell when the Kims opened them next spring.

At the side gate to the Kim estate, I looked out at the beautiful canyon. It lay spread out below, a tangle of twisted brush at least half a mile across. It would be easy to get lost in there.

April placed her thumb onto the biometric scanner. The gate began to swing open.

Then I heard a shout.

Behind us, Jae Woo was striding quickly towards us. His face looked hard and angry. The dwarf Mina was behind him, her hump rising and falling. She was holding a few pieces of the broken terra cotta statue—including the horse's head.

I didn't need to be a novelist to see the story here. Mina had discovered the microphone. And she had shown the microphone to Jae Woo. And Jae Woo was gunning for the tutor who'd brought the statue into his home.

And that tutor looked towards the spot where he'd parked his car. It wasn't even there. Mina had had it towed a few days earlier. April had said that her dad would have it finished by the weekend.

I was trapped.

"Run into the canyon," said April. "He hates getting dirty and won't follow you. Let me know what's going on as soon as you find out."

"I'll text you. Will you find my car?"

"I'll try," she said. "Hey, Jake."

Something in her voice made me stop. "What?"

"Thank you for helping me."

A thousand responses zinged through my head. None of them seemed right.

"You're welcome," I said. Then I turned and plunged into the brush.

FORTY-NINE

I scrambled down the steep side of the hill, mostly sliding. My shoes were caked with dirt within seconds. When it got too steep, I swung between manzanita bushes, my hands gripping the smooth reddish bark of the trunks, the succulent green leaves leaving a sticky residue on my hands.

Within five minutes, I was deep in the canyon. I paused behind an oak tree, breathing hard, and looked up. Jae Woo was standing at the lip of the canyon, hands on his hips.

He was looking at me.

It was too far to shout, but the trail of dust I'd kicked up probably had made it easy to follow me. I imagined how guilty this sudden escape must make me look, but the truth was that I was just as in the dark about the microphone as he was.

I turned and plunged deeper into the canyon. The air grew stiflingly hot. I crossed a dry creek bed, feeling the sticks crack beneath my feet. Somewhere in the weeds nearby, the ominous sound of a rattlesnake told me to get my feet back onto a path, so I did.

Fifteen minutes later, I looked back again. Jae Woo

looked a lot smaller now, but he was still there, on the lip of the canyon. I waited to see how long he would watch me. It took a couple more minutes, but finally he turned and headed back into his estate. The gate stayed open.

I kept walking further down the trail. I didn't have a clue where I was headed, except that it would probably spit me out at some point into a rich neighborhood with an ocean view. I passed a couple of hikers, nice skinny people in sunhats and walking poles who nodded at me through their smiling faces.

More than half an hour after I'd plunged into the canyon, I came out of it. There was a gate, a trash can, and a welcome sign facing the other way. Beyond lay a nice street with pretty houses and manicured lawns. I figured I'd walked at least a mile away from the Kim mansion.

Now I needed to get to Jarvis' office. I pulled out my phone to call a taxi. My phone read zero bars available. There was no signal here.

Dammit. It didn't surprise me. Rich people who live in the canyons of Los Angeles have this problem all the time, because mobile phone signals can't penetrate the hills. Many of them end up using landlines at home.

I would have to borrow someone's landline.

I stepped onto the street and peered around for a target. I spotted one. A middle-aged man was standing in his front yard, aiming a garden hose at a bed of flowers. He was wearing a Hawaiian shirt with shorts and velcro sandals. His toenails were yellowed and curled.

Not my first choice, but the quickest one.

"You look like a man with a telephone," I said.

He didn't even glance at me. "What tells you that?"

"You look like you're in touch with the world. Busy. A wheeler and dealer. Always be closing, right?"

He sneered. "I haven't pulled in a paycheck in three and a half years." He shook his head. "This goddamn economy."

"How're you meeting the mortgage on this little shack then?"

He swung towards me, sending the jet of water landing at my feet. "Say, whatever happened to foreplay? You just dive right in?"

"Only when I'm short on time. Right now, you're looking at six feet of witty banter begging for help. And I don't mean a slurp from your garden hose."

"What if I say no?"

"Then it's onto the next rich asshole."

That made him laugh. "Then I guess I'm your only hope, because none of these other assholes even answers their doors."

He went over to the faucet and turned off the garden hose. Then he went inside.

I went over to the faucet and turned it on again. Then I lifted the hose and tried to take a slurp. I soaked the whole front of my shirt.

He came back out with a cordless phone and saw me with his hose. "I knew you were thirsty. Feel free. My wife's upstairs naked and waiting too."

"No thanks, it's my day off," I said.

He tossed the phone to me. I dialed a taxicab, walked to the curb, and read the man's address to the dispatcher.

I clicked off and handed him the phone back and sat down on the sidewalk and waited.

"It's a hot day to be hiking in the canyon."

"Yeah."

"It wasn't your choice, was it?"

I shook my head.

He sucked on his pen. "I'm guessing that you walked from the other side. Probably from that estate there."

His finger was extended across the canyon towards the Kim mansion. It looked like a distant mirage in the hazy yellow heat.

"Nope," I lied.

"Then my binoculars need to be fixed."

I hadn't noticed them hanging around his neck.

He continued. "Kim's an odd duck," he said. "Inscrutable. The neighborhood rumor mill has been churning about him for years."

Something that tasted young and bitter welled up inside my mouth. "Nobody but good old-fashioned white-collar swindlers allowed up here, right?"

To my surprise, the man nodded. "Yes, we only like a certain type of dirt up here. But Kim over there, he's different."

I sat quietly. I didn't want to verify any of this man's guesses. Until I found out from Jarvis what was happening, it was better to avoid being associated with that house.

A couple minutes later, a taxicab rounded the bend. "You know," the man said, "I can't bear thinking this is the end of our conversation."

"All good things," I said, "must come to an end."

"But I'm unemployed. All I live for now is gossip."

As I slipped into the taxicab, he shouted. "Call me with details on Kim. You know I've got a phone."

I nodded at him as the vehicle started to head back down the hill. But the chances weren't likely.

FIFTY

The taxi pulled up in front of Jarvis' office. I paid the driver and told him to wait. Then I entered the long, nondescript office building.

Inside, I quickly found Jarvis' suite and knocked on the door. Nobody answered. I knocked a second time. Waited again. Then I tried the door handle. It was locked.

Something felt wrong. It was Friday at four o'clock pm. This was prime time for parents and students to be visiting a private college counselor's office. Especially in the fall, which Jarvis had said was his busy season.

I went down the hall to the building manager's office. I went inside and found an obese black man eating lunch in a tiny office. The edge of his desk was pressed horizontally into his gut, which spilled over onto the unrolled sandwich wrapper. He was wearing a blue custodian's uniform.

"Excuse me," I said, "do you know who has the keys to the offices?"

He didn't wait to swallow. "That's me."

"I need to get into the office of Kenneth Jarvis."

The custodian swallowed his sandwich. "I'm sorry, but that's not persuasive enough. Try harder."

"You sound like my mother."

He shook his head sadly. "Momma jokes already," he said. "And here we were, just getting to know each other."

"Listen," I said, "your flirting is getting me hot under the collar. Let's find a room together. Suite 324."

"Nice segue," said the custodian. He thumbed through his enormous ring of master keys. "Let's see. I got 322, 323 ... 325." He looked up. "I don't know what happened to 324. I musta left that one in my don't give-a-shit box."

I pulled out a twenty-dollar bill and laid it next to his sandwich wrapper. He looked up at me. "General Jackson killed lots of Florida natives."

"So what?"

"I'm one eighth Seminole."

This guy needed to show off that he was more than a custodian. It was annoying me. "And I'm seven-eighths pissed off."

He shrugged. "All white people look alike to me."

I took back the twenty-dollar bill and laid down a fifty in its place. He murmured approvingly. "General Grant, that's a man who could write. You ever read his memoirs?"

"I promise to write a book report if you'll stand up from that desk."

He finally did. He was the size of a compost heap. "This way," he said.

I followed him out of the office and back down the hall. His butt cheeks were a pair of huge slow-moving hams.

He stopped in front of Jarvis' suite. His fingers pulled out the same key ring. He chose a different one and inserted it into the lock and turned.

The door popped open. He stepped into Jarvis' office first. "Hey, you sure this is the right office?"

I craned my head, trying to see around his bulk. "There's a desk and a couple chairs and a refrigerator."

"Not anymore," he said.

He stepped aside, and I finally saw the office.

It was empty. *Completely* empty.

The secretary's desk was gone. The refrigerator, gone. The waiting room chairs, gone. Nothing but small dents left in the carpet.

I felt speechless.

I walked into Jarvis' private office, home to all his heavy mahogany furniture. That was all gone too. It couldn't have been easy to move.

But Jarvis had done it. He had packed up shop and split.

"Do you know when the last time he was here?"

The custodian was busy studying a fingernail. "Not without checking the security tapes. But General Grant doesn't buy you access to that. Were you supposed to meet him?"

"No."

I stood there, dazed. A pair of cable wires sprouted out of the corner of the room. The smell of modern office chemicals hung in the air.

"Hey, Jack, I don't have time to stand here all day handing you tissues," the custodian said. "Let's beat it." He hitched a thumb over his shoulder.

"Right," I said. I stepped back out into the hallway. The custodian stepped out behind me and shut the door and locked it.

"Come back any time," he said. "You're an important addition to my income now."

"We'll see."

He saluted me, then trudged slowly down the hallway. It was the only way he could walk.

I leaned against the wall and shut my eyes. I started thinking about Jarvis. I'd been dumped, without warning, without explanation, and probably without final payment— by a former friend who was very possibly part of a criminal syndicate himself. I couldn't think of any other reason for such a speedy anonymous departure.

The more I thought about it, the more furious I became. And the more furious I became, the more I had to find out what was really going on.

My next step would look incredibly stupid on paper, but it felt brilliant to my adrenalized mind.

I needed to go back to April's house.

There, I would tell Jae Woo everything. About finding the microphone, about how my panicked flight wasn't what it appeared to be, about how I was innocent of spying on his family. Then I would tell him about Jarvis' empty office. I would dissociate myself from Jarvis completely. Jae Woo was a reasonable man. He would understand.

I wouldn't ask about his business. That wasn't my concern. But I would also ask for the money that he owed me for living on premises for the last week. I hadn't forgotten about the money. Thad, the personal trainer, had warned me about that.

I walked out of the office complex. The heat of the day almost knocked me back on my heels. The world was telling me to go home, go to sleep, go away.

But I was angry now.

The same taxicab that had brought me here was parked under the shade of a tree in the corner of the lot. I walked over to it. The driver was asleep behind the wheel with the radio on.

I knocked on the roof, startling him awake, then slid into the back seat. "We're going back to Bel Air," I said.

FIFTY-ONE

On the ride back up into the wealthy hillside neighborhood, I took out my phone and dialed April's number.

It went immediately to a recorded message. But it wasn't her voicemail. It was the mechanized female voice of the phone company saying that the number had been disconnected.

I clicked off and stared with a beating heart at my own phone. Had someone messed with my contacts list when I wasn't looking? I dialed her number again, just in case, and got the same response.

My stomach had tied itself into a knot. This was getting weirder and weirder.

I directed the driver around the curves, past the modernist homes, past the cemented hillslope, up to the very front gate of the Kim estate. The fifteen-foot-high wall seemed higher than it ever had been.

I paid the driver and told him to wait. I peered around for a good piece of shade. A cleaning van was parked in the only one available, beneath a nearby oak, about fifty meters away. I pointed to the van and told the driver to park behind it.

This way I knew where to find him when I was ready to leave. It was purely practical. If things got ugly with Jae Woo inside, and if I needed to sprint out of the house and back to the street, I didn't want to be waiting around.

The taxi driver nodded, then pulled away. I watched him park behind the van.

I turned and walked up to the gate and pressed the call-box. A small buzz sounded. Nobody picked up. Mina was usually quick about that. I tried again. No response.

Ignoring the callbox, I pushed on the black iron gate. It didn't open. I hadn't expected it to.

A wise person would've called it quits right then and there, but my life has been full of roads less travelled. I decided scale the wall.

It wasn't my first time doing this. I'd executed wall climbs at my gym, under the eye of a trainer paid for by a film production company. But there had always been a harness around my waist. Here I had nothing but my fingers and toes.

I felt around the wall. It wasn't totally flat. Beneath the ivy, there were holes as well as bricks jutting out. Thank God for small miracles. There'd have been no way I could scale a smooth surface, at least not without a red spider costume.

I placed my left hand onto a brick hold, then my right toe into a hole. Then my left foot into a higher hole, and my right hand onto a higher brick hold. I felt ivy crunching inside my palm.

I repeated the process a few inches higher.

The important thing is to work quickly, and this didn't take long. I was fueled by curiosity and anger. In less than half a minute, I was perched on top of the wall, swinging my legs over, hanging by my fingertips, and then dropping to the grass on the other side.

Five meters isn't an easy drop, but at least the grass was springy. I laid on my side for a bit, shaking the sting out of my ankles, mouthing curses. Then I pulled myself up to a sitting position, slowly got to my feet, and found the front walk a few feet away.

As I limped down the walk, the sunlight that had been dappling my arms quickly disappeared. I felt the same dark chill rise up my spine that I had felt on my very first visit. Sweat dripped into my eyes as the tunnel of trees grew more and more claustrophobic.

Then the tunnel ended, and I was looking at the elaborate formal English garden, the sundial, the ring of brass arrows. Looming over the gardens, the Kim mansion seemed even darker, even more cloaked in secrecy. I decided that the architect must've been a sorcerer.

I stepped around the buried kimchi pots and rang the doorbell. I could hear the heavy ding-dong echoing inside the house. Mina was going to be surprised to see me. I would've rehearsed an opening line, if she'd understood English.

But nobody answered the door. I was just standing on the front porch like an idiot. I rang the doorbell again and listened for movement. Nothing sounded inside.

I quietly circled around the house to the side entrance, the one that led into the kitchen, the one where Jae Woo had greeted me that first night I was wearing my bathrobe. I pushed on the door.

It was open.

This was an uncharacteristic mistake. I mean, this

family literally locked up their own daughter. An open door meant something was seriously wrong.

I stepped into the kitchen and looked around. On a cutting board were several half-chopped radishes. A knife lay next to them, its blade wet with juice.

They'd been here recently—and they'd left in a hurry.

I tiptoed into the main foyer. Nothing seemed disturbed or out of place. I peered into Jae Woo's office, the place where he'd fed me drinks, patted me down, and railed against his lazy daughter. Nothing looked any different.

I walked down the hall to April's study room. "April?" I shouted. "It's Jake. What happened to your phone?"

No response. I looked inside her study. She wasn't there. Nothing was disturbed, though. Her bookbag was in its customary place. Her desk looked the same. Her cell phone was in its charger, where she'd placed it before starting the diagnostic test that morning. And the broken pieces of the terra cotta statue were still on the floor, just as we'd left them.

Then I noticed that one item was missing. Her laptop.

The lectern on which she normally kept it was empty. The cord was gone too. It'd been there this morning. I'd been reading her college application essay on it.

I left April's study and went up the stairs to the second floor. I visited my bedroom.

Everything had been strewn across the floor. I knew it would be. Jae Woo had gone through every piece of my clothing, every toiletry, every book. But I hadn't brought much, and nothing was suspect.

I really couldn't blame him. If I'd invited someone to live in my house, and if that someone had smuggled a microphone inside a statue, I'd probably search his stuff too.

I collected my items, stuffed them into my duffel bag,

and slung it over my shoulder. Then I went down the hall to April's room. There was one more thing I wanted to check.

The door was closed. I knocked, then said her name. There was no response. That wasn't any surprise. I pushed inside.

Her clothing was strewn across the floor. There was a large rectangular impression upon the blankets of her bed. It told me that something had been there recently. My guess was a suitcase.

What would tell the real story was Churchill, the stuffed teddy bear that lived underneath her pillow. I lifted the pillow.

Nothing but sheets.

I put the pillow back down. That sealed it. This family had evacuated the house—possibly for good.

I left her bedroom and ran downstairs. Fear had seized my heart. If Jae Woo saw fit to evacuate his family on a moment's notice, then who knew what group of people was headed this way. And I would be the only person left to greet the coming terror. Coming back here had been a terrible decision. So had working for Jarvis. I should've known better than to do either.

I ran through the house, out the kitchen door, back across the front yard, past the sundial and the buried kimchi pots, and through the tunnel of trees that led to the front gate. The wall loomed high before me.

I saw my next steps. I would climb the wall, jump into the waiting taxi, ride home, head out for a sunset surf—and then forget that April Kim had ever existed. I'd take the hit on the money. It was worth it. My marginal existence as a marginal actor had never felt so attractive.

I ran up to the ivy-covered wall and threw my duffel bag over. Then I placed my toes and hands in the right places. I pulled myself up even more quickly than I had the first time. It's easy when you're juiced on adrenaline.

At the top, I threw my leg over until I was straddling the wall, then looked out onto the street.

The taxicab was gone. The cleaning van's back doors were open.

A group of fifteen people were looking up at me.

They were standing in a semi-circle around the bottom of the wall. Each of them wore a bright-yellow windbreaker. I'd seen those windbreakers before, on the set of a police procedural drama.

These people were from the federal government.

And in the middle of the group, wearing a yellow windbreaker, was Jarvis.

FIFTY-TWO

Jarvis cupped his mouth with one hand and made a come-here gesture with the other. "Come on down, Jake," he said. "We're not going to hurt you."

He pointed to another agent. She was holding my duffel bag. "We caught your bag."

I saw that everyone was carrying a weapon. Then I noticed that three different men had separated from the group, fanned out, and were watching me like predatory birds. It was their job.

"All right," I said.

There was no point to resisting. I twisted around, lowered myself down the wall until I was hanging by my fingertips, then dropped onto the grass. The three men pounced on me as soon as I hit the ground. They rolled me onto my belly and put the Flexicuffs on my wrists. It felt like a scene in a movie—but this was real.

Then they hooked their hands under my armpits and hauled me to my feet. My ankles were stinging, and now I could feel the plastic ties cutting off the circulation in my wrists.

"You guys have got a feathery touch," I said.

"Lots of practice," one said.

"I'm not guilty of anything."

"Nobody said you were."

"Then why the wrist kisses?"

Jarvis' voice cut in. "I ordered it. No special treatment, Jake. You were breaking and entering."

I hung my head. He was right. Then I looked up. "A college counselor? Really?"

He shrugged. "It was a good cover."

"So you never worked at Harvard's admissions office."

"Nah," he replied. "And considering you never graduated, I'd say that Jae Woo got totally ripped off. Come on, let's talk."

He took me by the arm to the shaded part of a nearby curb. He sat me down. I was crouched with my knees nearly up to my ears, and my arms pinned behind my back. I felt like an arrested frog.

Then he went back to his team. I watched him give a couple of directions, speak into a radio, point at the wall, make a circular motion. It looked like a raid. Seven people split off from the group and ran around the property until they were out of sight.

Then Jarvis returned and sat next to me on the curb.

"I only have a couple minutes, and there's a lot that I can't tell you," he said.

"You're full of good news."

He wisely ignored my gibe. "So here's the truth. I work for the FBI. My team was assigned to Kim's house. We were supposed to gather intelligence."

"So these people are all FBI?"

He shook his head no. "Just five of us. Four are from Customs, plus a couple of DEA. At our other raid sites, there's even more. Sixteen agencies in total. It's a huge operation."

"What's it for?"

"Transnational smuggling. Jae Woo was part of a syndicate of people who were bringing counterfeit money from China into the Port of Los Angeles. We have reason to think he was shipping drugs too."

I didn't know what to say. The fact of Jae Woo's crime wasn't surprising, but the scale of the crime was.

"I didn't know China makes—"

Jarvis cut me off. "China is just a middleman. It's really North Korea. We've known about it for years. They bring the goods across the frozen Tumen River into Manchuria, then down to Shanghai, then load them into shipping containers to Los Angeles."

"How can we allow that?"

He looked at me like I was new. "Only two percent of shipping containers entering the United States ever get inspected, Jake."

That was news to me. Still, I thought about Jae Woo's unnerving demeanor. It would totally be in keeping with what I knew about North Korea. Militaristic, reptilian, total lacking in self-awareness. Maybe Jae Woo had been a North Korean citizen, one who'd been allowed to "escape", to facilitate the black market money that was keeping the pathetic regime afloat.

But this was all speculation from an unemployed actor sitting handcuffed on a curb in Bel Air.

"Again, I'm sorry that I had to lie to you," said Jarvis. "But please keep in mind that you did really help April. And it turns out that you're quite good at tutoring."

"How the hell do you know?" I said miserably.

"Because I was listening."

He had a queer smile on his face. Then I remembered the microphones. They had picked up everything.

"Your methods are unusual—but you achieve results. In fact, we in the office had a little side bet going whether April would get a perfect score on a practice test before her test date. Thanks. I won fifty dollars."

I felt used and abused.

Jarvis must've seen the pain on my face. He reached into his pocket and pulled out his wallet and removed a few bills and stuffed them into my shirt pocket. "Here," he said, "two hundred from our slush fund. You sure won't be getting any money from the Kim family."

I felt even more embarrassed. He'd known all about me working privately, around his so-called company. The joke was entirely on me.

"Did I cause this raid?" I said. "When I broke the terra cotta statue this morning?"

Jarvis shook his head. "No, but you accelerated it by a few hours. We were just about ready to move anyways." He chucked my shoulder. "Be more careful around fine art, okay?"

"Talk to the girl who tackled me," I said. "Where do you think her dad took her?"

He grew tight-lipped. "I can't discuss that. But you can probably imagine that someone as crafty as Jae Woo had made an escape plan."

"Yeah."

"It's not going to work. We're going to catch him." Jarvis held a faraway look of determination in his eye. I had newfound respect for my friend from college.

Then he snapped out of it. He pulled a small knife from his belt and reached behind me and cut off the plastic ties.

My arms fell forward, along my sides. I rubbed my wrists until the feeling started to return.

"I have something to tell you," he said. "You weren't here today."

He held my eye until I understood.

"Okay."

"Repeat it," he said.

"I wasn't here today," I said.

"You walked across the canyon, caught the taxi, and went straight home."

"Absolutely."

"Now you're going to do a little more walking. Listen closely." Jarvis pointed down the street. "You're going to walk down to the bottom of the hill and turn right. In two blocks you'll see a man sitting inside an unmarked Ford Taurus. He's part of our team. Get into the backseat. He'll take you to get your car."

I'd forgotten all about that. Jae Woo had sent my car to a mechanic to get fixed. What a fool I'd been to trust him.

"How do you know where—"

He didn't bother to let me finish. "Lojack."

"On *my* car?"

"Of course. You were part of the operation. We've been watching the mechanic for days. The guy is dirty but scared as hell. He's fixing your car under the watchful gaze of my assistant." He doffed an imaginary hat. "Courtesy of the agency. For your service."

Jarvis was using his leverage to get a free repair for me. That was thoughtful. It looked like I would be getting something out of this, after all. "Your family is getting a nice fruit basket at Christmas, Jarvis."

He shook his head. "I don't have a family. I don't even live in Los Angeles."

"But that picture—"

He shook his head again. "That's cover, my friend." He stuck out his hand. "You've been a big help."

"One more question," I said.

He lowered his hand. "Yes."

"Why did you use me? Why couldn't you have used one of your agents?"

He smiled. "We did. We tried seven different people. Anybody with the remotest tie to the intelligence community heard about this."

"So?"

"April fired all of them. You were the only tutor she liked."

That was a nice thing to know. It must've registered on my face, because Jarvis said, "Forget about her, Jake. You did your job, it's over. She'll survive."

My old college buddy stuck his hand out again. This time I reached out and shook it. We stayed like that for a second longer than usual. "Hey," he said, "the eagle flies at morning light."

The answer caught in my throat. I couldn't answer him. It didn't feel good to have invented The Owl and the Pigeons, not anymore. We'd both changed too much.

"All right," he said. "I understand."

Then he turned away and walked across the street and rejoined the rest of his team.

Confused and exhausted, I trudged down the hill towards the waiting vehicle.

FIFTY-THREE

The ride from Bel Air to Koreatown was slow, owing to Friday rush hour. We sat in a five-mile-long line of outbound traffic on Sunset Boulevard.

The driver was a young guy about my age whose lips seemed to have been sewn shut. Maybe that's too judgmental. After all, I didn't say anything to him either. I was too tired.

Nearly two hours later, he pulled into a tight alley near 9th and James Wood in Koreatown. The sun was low in the sky now, and the alley was growing dark.

He parked along the wall, turned off the engine, and pulled the stitches out of his mouth. "Follow me," he said.

I stepped out of the car and followed him into an open garage. Inside was a small, thuggish Korean man wearing a greasy pair of coveralls. He was buffing the hood of a car.

Then I realized that it was *my* car.

A woman walked over to greet me. She had broad shoulders and the boring hairstyle of somebody's mother. I recognized her immediately. It was the woman who'd been pretending to be Jarvis' secretary.

"Hey," she said.

"I've been dying to tell you something," I replied.

"What?"

"You're a terrible typist. Do you want lessons?"

She didn't think this was funny in the least. "I didn't spend twenty years in the agency to play secretary to some young kid like Jarvis. Jesus, *I* should've played the college counselor. It would've been much more believable, don't you think?"

Her anger was oddly familiar to me. She sounded like an actor bitter about being passed over—only she was an FBI agent.

"So you were miscast," I said. "At least you had a part. Get over yourself."

Her face narrowed. "I can have this guy do some really bad things to your car. And he's quite willing."

The mechanic had stopped rubbing. He was glaring at us with hatred in his eyes. She pointed at the hood. He started buffing again.

She turned back to me and looked down at her clipboard. "So you've got a new rack-and-pinion, fixed the catalytic converter, four new tires, yadda yadda. Here, read it for yourself." She unclipped the bill and shoved it at me.

I looked down the itemized list of repairs. It was long. The tab probably would've run three thousand dollars at a regular mechanic. "Jesus, it really needed a lot of work."

Her nostrils flared as she handed my keys to me. "See, getting used isn't so bad, is it? It's good to be on the outside sometimes. Better than the inside."

She was burning with resentment and jealousy. I'd let her burn out.

"You're a real princess," I said.

"Word to the wise," she said, "you might want to get the brakes checked by somebody else. I'm just saying."

That was a good idea, and I told her so. I jangled the keys in my hand and walked over to my car. The mechanic stopped buffing. He stepped back from my car with barely disguised fury in his eyes. It would be good to leave this place.

I slipped behind the wheel. The interior had been cleaned. I considered asking for some lemon scent, then decided not to push my luck. I turned the ignition key. The engine turned over immediately. It hadn't run this well in years.

I rolled down my window. "Tell Jarvis thanks."

"Tell him yourself," said the woman.

I put the car into drive, then pulled out of the garage and pulled away down the alley.

FIFTY-FOUR

I arrived back at my apartment an hour later. It was too late to surf.

At my front door, a package was waiting for me on the mat. It was thin. It had been delivered via UPS. My upstairs neighbor had signed for it. She always does that for me.

I held it in my hands and looked at the return address. It read *L. Sapelstein*. The address read Beverly Hills.

My agent. These must be the breakup papers. This was very strange. Nobody in the entertainment business ever did something like this. They preferred to let your ego wither up and blow away into a desert of silence.

I ripped open the package and pulled out the papers within. I read through them. They weren't breakup papers at all.

I was holding a new two-year contract. The appropriate signature lines had been marked by little sticky colored arrows.

And there was a post-it note on the front of the document. In spidery, unattractive handwriting was the following message: *Ready to turn up the heat. –Lew.*

I tried to suppress a smile, but it came out anyways. I didn't love acting, but the craft was like a girlfriend who I'd been with too long to dump. And now I was going to get a second shot. No withering in the desert of silence for my ego. No exile to community theater.

It was back to my previous life.

I unlocked my apartment and went inside and took a shower and laid down on my bed. I hadn't been here for over a week. It felt uncomfortable somehow. I decided that the discomfort was in my mind. It was revved up. If I were an engine, I would've redlined by now.

April Kim. I couldn't stop thinking about what might happen to her. Here she was, on the cusp of giving her best SAT performance ever—a potential perfect score—and yet she was being whisked away by her criminal father to an undisclosed location. With a large team of federal agents on their trail.

It wasn't fair to her. She'd had a lot of advantages in life, but she hadn't chosen her father. And if she didn't take the SAT, it would destroy her dream of attending Harvard.

Then I realized that there was something I could do. This would be my swan song to April Kim, the very last time I would help her.

It would require a small favor from Jarvis, however. He would understand.

I reached for my phone and dialed Jarvis' number.

FIFTY-FIVE

SIX MONTHS LATER

I'm floating just off the Hermosa Beach pier, wearing my shorty wetsuit. My surfboard feels good between my legs. On shore, it's a gorgeous natural day. The springtime buds, the blooming purple jacarandas, the scent of jasmine. Fresh growth.

Out here, though, in the lineup with a hundred other hopeful surfers, it's the smell of neoprene and suntan lotion and briny seawater. I don't really know why I'm out here today. The sets of waves are weak and inconsistent. There are too many people in the lineup.

I recognize a couple of local thugs here. They tip their chins at me. I nod back but have to swallow my distaste. I've seen these guys get violent when outsiders try to come in.

A halfway decent wave arrives, but it looks like a ride in a Cadillac today. I'm feeling generous and decide to let it pass. I turn to face shore and watch about thirty people all vying to drop in at the same time.

One of them is a girl, petite, wearing another shorty wetsuit. Her hair is black and slicked straight back. She looks young.

I watch the girl as she barely gets up before her legs go wobbly and she pitches over into the water. She's a total newbie. I'd been there once. Getting up to your feet is the hardest thing to master.

But the guy who'd dropped in next to her is one of the thuggish locals. Even from behind the wave, I can tell that his board is aiming for her head. I hold my breath, anticipating a collision, but thankfully he bails instead.

But now he's pissed off. I see their heads pop up out of the white foam. She's trying to climb back onto her board, but he's grabbing her feet and yanking her off her board. She's kicking back at him. Now he's yelling at her.

It's getting ugly. I knew it would.

Jake Logan's not a fighter, but neither is he the kind of guy to allow injustice to go unconfronted. I lean forward onto my belly and paddle over with a few quick windmill strokes.

"You don't want this," I tell him.

"You butt out," he says, without looking.

"Seriously," I say.

He whirls with clenched fists, then recognizes me. "Oh, Jake. What's up? Sorry."

He mounts his board and paddles off. I have a decent reputation here. And it doesn't take much to scare off a bully.

The girl is looking up at me from the water. I see right away that she's Asian. Then I see something that I can't believe.

It's April Kim. My student. I had forgotten about her until last week.

"Jake," she says.

"No way," I say. "You're *not* here."

She pulls herself up onto her board. "Why not?"

"Because your father—"

"—is going to federal prison? Because my school wouldn't let me graduate, or even sit in class, after he was arrested? Because my life is completely screwed?"

She blows salt water out of her nasal cavity. I look the other way while she does it.

"Believe it or not," she says, "I'm still alive, even if people don't want to believe it."

"Come to the shore and let's talk."

"I don't need to talk."

"Well," I said, "I'll be waiting right by that lifeguard station when you get tired. And I've got something you want to see."

I paddle in and rip the leash from my ankle. I toss the surfboard onto the sand and sat down. There are some teenage girls looking at me nearby. They'd seen me scare off the thug. I nod at them and wait for April.

I'll give her this much. It takes her longer to tire out than I'd predicted. Forty minutes later she finally drags her board out of the surf. She gets it about ten feet up the sand before she gave up. It was no surprise. Her arms are like a pair of matchsticks.

I stand up and help her drag it a few more feet, safely out of reach of the surf. She picks up her bag and finds a bottle of water and drinks all of it in a single swallow. Then she wipes her lips and looks at me.

"What?"

"You came here to find me," I say.

"No, I didn't."

"You want to tell me something. I can see it."

She can't meet my eyes. That's how I know I'd hit the nail on the head. "You *wish*," she says.

"Tell me, April."

"Nope."

I laugh inside. "Okay. I'll guess instead. You came surfing because you wanted to tell me that you never took the SAT because of your dad's arrest."

"Wrong."

"So you did take it—but you blew it."

Her lip quivers a little bit. Bingo.

I shake my head. "So you never got to show the world your perfect score."

"So what?" she finally bursts out. "I don't care what some college thinks of me. Or you either. Now since you're so smart, what else are you going to tell me about myself?"

I think for a moment. "I'm guessing that you didn't get into Harvard. In fact, I'm betting you didn't even apply to any college."

She looks at me like a wounded animal. "How did you know *that*?"

"Because you need letters of recommendation to get into private schools, and the teachers at Chandler-Beacon were probably barred from helping you. If they'd even wanted to."

April drops to the sand. She put her head between her hands. Her whole body heaved. I realized that she was sobbing.

I crouch next to her and put my hand on her back. "Don't worry."

She lifts her face. I try not to shrink back in horror. She's an ugly crier.

"How can I not worry? I'm not going to *college*! My life is *ruined*!"

"Because," I say, "I have something to give you."

"What?"

"I need to get it from my apartment."

"I'm not going into your apartment."

I snort. "You wouldn't be allowed inside anyways. It's a drama-free zone. Stay here, April. It's only three blocks away. I'll be right back."

I lift my surfboard and walk up the sand with it tucked underneath my arm. I hike up the sidewalk to my front door, lean my surfboard against the wall, unlock it, and go inside.

The thing I want to give her is sitting on my desk. It's a full-sized envelope. I'd received it in the mail but hadn't opened it. I black out the return address, so it won't ruin the surprise.

I go back outside and walk down the sidewalk, back to the beach. She is still sitting there, with her narrow back to me, looking out at the ocean.

I sit down next to her again and hand her the envelope. I don't need to say anything.

She peers at the front. "Why is it addressed to me, care of you?"

"Open it."

She looks suspicious. Still, she rips open the envelope. A sheaf of papers fall out, all different colors.

"Read the first one," I say.

The one on the front is addressed to Miss April Kim. I look over her shoulder, just to be sure it says what I think it should say. *The California State University has received your application and is pleased to offer you a position in the fall semester...*

Her jaw drops. "I'm going to college?"

I nod. "It ain't Harvard, but Cal State doesn't require either SATs or letters of recommendation."

"How did you—"

"Jarvis. He gave me your Social Security number."

"But the essay—"

"There wasn't one."

"My transcript?"

"I called in a favor at your school. Sam, senior class president, did it."

"But Sam *hates* me."

"Exactly. That's why he was happy to send you to Cal State Northridge."

She clutches her stomach. "Oh God. CSUN. That's in the valley."

"Do you have a better choice?"

She bows her head. For the first time, I can see true humility in her. Then she looks up.

"Why do you have to be *right* all the time?"

"I'm an actor," I say. "I just pretend to be right. Sometimes it hits the mark."

"You're not an actor," she replies. "You're a tutor, Jake Logan. And I'm lucky that I met you."

I hold up my hand for a high five. She slaps it so hard that my hand stings.

GAMBLING
FOR GEORGETOWN

A JAKE LOGAN
PRIVATE TUTOR
MYSTERY

J.A. JERNAY

GAMBLING FOR GEORGETOWN

"Something to drink?" the old priest said. "I have wine or scotch."

"Scotch."

He looked at me with cunning eyes. "That's a serious drink."

"I never could tell a joke," I said.

I watched him reach into the drawer of his desk, remove a bottle of Laphroaig, and unscrew the top. He poured a finger into a small glass and handed it to me.

I sipped the heavy liquid and felt my guard lower. God, I was an easy mark. "Nothing for you?"

The old man replaced the bottle but didn't answer. "Have a seat."

I sat down in the chair across from him. Behind the desk, the old man leaned back and laced his hands behind his head. "So, Jake, here's what I know. Apparently you tried to rape one of my boys."

I felt my blood pressure rise. Coming here had been a terrible mistake. "No, I did not try to—"

He silenced me with the wave of a hand. It had a strange power. I immediately shut up.

"Then," he continued, "because you're nosy, you waited outside Michael's home tonight. You trailed him across the city to this address. You come sneaking in here like some sort of goddamn cat burglar. And now you're drinking my good Scotch."

I set down my drink. "You poured it. And I didn't sneak anywhere—"

The hand shushed me again. I was starting to hate that hand.

"We'll discuss you a bit more later," he said. "First, tell me what you think is happening in that backroom."

"They're playing blackjack," I replied.

"Tell me more," he said. "Be more specific."

This felt like a classroom. I shifted uncomfortably in my seat. "Well, you're teaching them how to gamble."

"Incorrect," he said. "Only gamblers gamble. I'm teaching the boys how to count."

The priest's face had lit up with wicked delight. A twitch crooked up the corner of his mouth. It looked like a crocodile trying to smile.

"Really?" I said.

"Really."

This was no revelation. What I hadn't figured out was why this old man had a vested interest in doing so, and his relationship to them.

He seemed to guess my thoughts. "I'm their math teacher," he said.

"Really?" I said again.

He nodded. "Hard to believe?"

Yes and no. Instead, I asked the burning question. "Why? Why would you teach them how to count cards?"

The old man looked me squarely in the eye. "Because these kids can't afford college."

That was no surprise. College tuitions had been rising at three times the rate of inflation, to the point where even public universities were getting pricey. The days of affordable higher education seemed to have passed.

Then the pieces began to fall into place. "Ah," I said, "you teach them how to count cards at blackjack. Then they use those winnings to pay for college."

He nodded. "Exactly."

I laughed. "I imagine the IRS might want to know about this."

His eyes leveled with mine. "It's all completely protected. Nobody can touch me." Then he waited a beat. "And you can't touch me either. Not even if I were a seventeen-year-old boy."

My nostrils flared. The old man wouldn't let this alone. And a priest had no right to be making those types of joks. "Look, that is not what happened—"

"Sure it was," he said. "The boys told me."

I stopped talking. His eyes were dancing merrily behind his thick lenses. I got the sense that he was yanking my chain, that I was the butt of some sick practical joke.

Then I thought of all the hundreds of other things I could be doing right now. Like reading, sleeping, making out with a new girlfriend. Instead I was getting sucked into a shady sting operation that could lead to a ten-year stint at state prison.

"This has been very interesting," I said, setting down the glass, "but it's my bedtime."

"Don't go," he said.

"Why not?"

A look of pain crossed his face. "Because we want you on our team, Jake."

I stopped. That was interesting, but my curiosity was going to destroy me one of these days if I didn't put a lid on it. Besides, I didn't know anything about how card counters operated. He could be setting me up to be a patsy. I could end up testifying in front of a grand jury.

"That's very nice of you," I said, "but I'm just an actor."

He smiled. "That's perfect. We need someone who can play various roles."

"But I don't know how to count cards," I said. "I barely even know how to play blackjack as it is."

He grew frustrated. "You don't have to know how to count cards. That's what the kids are for. All you have to do is sweep in like a high roller, watch the kids' signs, place a few big bets, and act happy when you scoop up a pile of cash."

I drained the glass and stood up. "Thanks for the Scotch."

"You're leaving?"

"I never should've come here tonight."

The priest looked disappointed. "So you won't even hear my offer?"

I shook my head. "Don't worry—my lips are sealed. I don't even want to know your name."

I saluted him, then turned and left the office and crossed the plaza and exited the iron door back to the street.

Michael's mystery had finally been explained. Now that I knew what he was doing at night, I was looking forward to leaving it all behind.

PLOTWORKS PUBLISHING

Visit Plotworks Publishing and discover a new series by J.A. Jernay—the Cosmo Bennett Mapping Thrillers!

Turn the page for another sneak peek—

J.A. JERNAY
BOUNDARY

A COSMO BENNETT MAPPING THRILLER

FROM *THE* AUTHOR OF *THE* AINSLEY WALKER
GEMSTONE TRAVEL MYSTERY SERIES

BOUNDARY

Cosmo and his assistant Noah shuffled down the dirt shoulder of the boulevard in the midday heat, sweating and miserable.

Each was lost in his own thoughts. Cosmo dreamed of hitting a heavy punching bag at his gymnasium. Noah dreamed of passing level nineteen of Operation Earlobe, an obscure RPG he'd abandoned last semester.

The morning's meeting had been a complete bust.

"I don't think we should continue," said Cosmo finally.

Noah didn't respond, but Cosmo took no notice. He continued: "I don't think anybody here takes our task seriously. I don't think this propaganda map was as influential as they say. I don't think this map has driven the civil unrest. I think social media and centuries of tribal warfare are more to blame for the unrest than anything else."

He looked over at Noah, waiting for a response. "What about you?"

The graduate assistant came back from his reverie. "Huh?"

"Did you hear anything I said?"

"No."

"I was just saying this is pointless and we should go home."

"I don't have a problem with that."

They arrived at Vida e Caffe. It was a chain café, with hundreds of similar franchises scattered across the southern half of the African continent. The branding was modern and inviting. A hundred people sat beneath umbrellas at small tables on the large outdoor patio.

An arm was waving at them. It was Christopher, their fixer, a cup of tea on a ceramic saucer in front of him. Two other cups awaited them.

"Hello sirs," he said. "I ordered us all a rooibos. It's a vanilla tea that is extraordinary."

Cosmo and Noah pulled out the chairs and sat down. The driver quickly sussed out that something was wrong.

"It was a bad meeting?" he said quietly.

"Yes," said Cosmo, "there was no progress made."

"I'm very sorry."

Cosmo sighed. "I think we have to leave."

The fixer looked confused. "But you just sat down—"

"The country," he clarified. "We have to leave Faba-jouti. We can't seem to do any good here."

Christopher looked crestfallen. "I do understand your frustration."

Noah said, "If it's okay with you, we'd probably like to just get in the car and go back to the hotel."

The fixer rediscovered his manners. "Of course, as you wish—"

"But we'd love to try the tea first—" added Cosmo.

"You two enjoy the rooibos," said Christopher, "while I fetch the car. The parking lot is very jammed and it will take quite a while to remove. I've already paid the bill."

Before they could object, the driver had shot to his feet. He clapped Cosmo on the shoulder and left the patio. They watched him cross the boulevard to an off-street parking area that was crammed tightly with vehicles. On his approach, the attendant began shifting other vehicles.

Noah sipped the tea. "This does taste really good. I don't drink enough tea."

"I like tea," said Cosmo. He sipped from the cup. "This one is good."

"What's your favorite?" asked Noah.

"Maybe pu'er."

"That one's bitter, right?"

"Yeah. It's fermented."

"What about Earl Grey?"

"A cliché."

"I think I'm more of a fruity tea guy," said Noah.

Cosmo nodded. "Yeah, they have their charms."

"You ever try chamomile?"

"It's good for sleeping," said Cosmo, "but otherwise it's—"

His comment was cut short by a massive fireball that erupted from the parking lot across the street.

In a split second, Cosmo and Noah instinctively rolled off their chairs and onto the ground beneath their table. Their eyes met. Each was filled with terror.

Then the shock of the overpressure hit. Cosmo felt the force of the blast wave hit the left side of his body. The highly compressed air rattled the left side of his skull. It even sent his lips and cheeks flapping to the right.

The initial sound of the explosion was deafening, but

that was soon replaced by a symphony of falling destruction. A thousand pieces of metal, plastic, glass, and upholstery rained down upon the boulevard, the grass, the other cars.

A shower of tiny shrapnel hit on the patio of the cafe. One hit Noah in the hand and sizzled his flesh. He shook it off.

They waited another few seconds for the shrapnel rain to end. Then Cosmo and Noah lifted their heads.

The patio of the café was transformed into pandemonium. The patrons started to pull themselves up from the ground and flee out to the street and in the opposite direction. The street itself was coming alive with panicked people running in every direction.

"What the actual—" said Noah.

"Christopher!" interrupted Cosmo. "What about Christopher?"

He scrambled up to his feet. Without waiting for Noah, he sprinted out of the café and across the boulevard, weaving through the stopped cars. The air was acrid with chemicals and the heat had somehow intensified even further.

The parking lot was a field of wreckage. The bomb had exploded in the middle of the space, shredding every vehicle and person within twenty meters. Pieces of concrete and metal and glass had been blown across the scene.

"Christopher!" he shouted again. "Christopher! Don't do this!"

He saw a shoe with a foot still in it. He saw a red string of guts entangled in a hubcap. A wave of nausea gripped his stomach. He covered his nose with his t-shirt and backed away.

He tripped backwards over a piece of metal, stumbled, and fell to the ground.

That's when he saw it.

A long strip of shredded fabric. A yellow-and-green printed tropical shirt.

It was bloody and torn.

Cosmo turned his head and retched onto the asphalt. All the tea he'd just drank came out.

He somehow pulled himself to his feet and staggered back to the café. Noah was waiting at the far corner, on the sidewalk, pacing frantically.

"So?"

"I found him," said Cosmo. He forced the next words out. "A little bit."

Noah's face went white. "Oh my God."

Cosmo didn't say anything. He just gripped Noah by the upper arm. "Walk with me. And don't look back."

The pair moved briskly down the boulevard, away from the scene. People were running past them, mouths open, eyes full of fear, but Cosmo maintained a steady pace. His face betrayed an intense desire to appear as normal as possible.

"So we're just going to leave the scene?" said Noah.

"Yep."

"Why?"

"Don't make me answer that, Noah."

"I think we should talk to the police, cooperate, tell them everything—"

"In a different country," Cosmo replied, "in a different scenario, you'd be right. But not here, not now."

Noah looked back over his shoulder at the scene.

"Look straight ahead," Cosmo said through his teeth, "and listen to me. Our Mercedes is gone. Christopher is ... gone."

"Shit—"

"And I'm going to suggest something else that could blow your mind."

"What?"

"It's possible that we were the intended target."

"That's insane."

"Is it?"

"How do you know?"

"I don't. But it's a possibility. Here's another one. It's possible that we are going to be used as scapegoats. We were the last people seen eating with Christopher. Do you want to be put in a Fabajouti jail on suspicion of a crime?"

They walked for another half minute in silence. Behind them, the chaos grew distant.

"Where are we going?" Noah said finally.

"Back to the hotel."

"And then?"

"We're leaving, like we planned."

"We're not going home, are we?" said Noah.

Cosmo's mouth grew hard and his jaw jutted out. He stared straight forward at an invisible point on the horizon. "No, we're not."

PLOTWORKS PUBLISHING

And be sure to read J.A. Jernay's best-known series—the Ainsley Walker Gemstone Travel Mysteries!

Turn the page for a final sneak peek—

THE

URUGUAY AMETHYST

AN AINSLEY WALKER
GEMSTONE TRAVEL MYSTERY

J.A. JERNAY

THE URUGUAY AMETHYST

Ainsley pulled the backseat door closed. Her driver's eyes looked at her in the rearview mirror.

"Where can I take you?" Oswaldo asked in Spanish.

"Back to Tabarez," she said.

He nodded, and they pulled away from the curb. Ainsley studied him in the mirror. His jaw was set firmly. She decided to see what she could learn from him.

"Do you like working for Tabarez?" she said.

"Yes," he said. Nothing else.

Of course he wouldn't comment on his employer. She decided to stick to facts.

"Oswaldo, after lunch I will need you to help me take a very large package to this address." She handed him the paper with Bernabé's address. "Can you find this place?"

He read the address and nodded. Not a word. Ainsley was beginning to wonder if he was a bit simple.

The car was slicing down La Rambla, and Ainsley contented herself with staring out the window, at the blurring breakwall and at the choppy brown water of the delta.

The sky was bright blue and the clouds puffy and white and a chill wind was blowing again.

It was mesmerizing. She wrapped her coat around herself more tightly and snuggled in.

Then she woke up to Oswaldo touching her knee. The vehicle had stopped. She was outside Tabarez's house.

Ainsley emerged from the vehicle and buttoned the top collar of her coat. "It's so cold here," she said.

Oswaldo didn't respond. Conversationally, there was no difference between her driver and a piece of drywall. She decided to just issue him orders instead. It would save both of them a lot of trouble.

"Stay here until I return."

He lit a cigarette and looked straight ahead.

Slinging her purse over her shoulder, Ainsley walked alone towards the house. Her stomach was twisting itself into anxious knots. Partly because of El Árbol Negro, partly because she was so hungry.

And nervous. She was about to enjoy homemade *ñoquis* in a private dining room with an extremely wealthy and attractive man who may or may not have refused to sleep with her, even after she'd thrown herself at him. Why did she have to black out on *that* night of *all* nights? And now he was going to sell her a famous amethyst after telling her its secret history.

This felt too good to be true.

The copper gate was rolled wide open. Ainsley cocked her head. That was strange, given the value of the contents inside the mansion.

She stepped through the open gate onto the driveway, then moved into the manicured yard. It made her heart sing again. She touched the bougainvillea, listened to the branches clacking in the breeze from the estuary.

Then she rang the front doorbell and waited. The slab of wood before her was exquisite. Spirals and whorls had been dug into its surface, like the enormous thumbprint of a criminal.

There was no response. That was weird. Heinrik was the epitome of the efficient manservant. He should've been there in a flash.

She rang the doorbell again, then turned and surveyed the landscaping. Water was trickling from some unseen fountain. She couldn't find it. An invisible bird sang crookedly from the branches of a tall ash. She couldn't find that either. A sinking feeling filled her stomach.

Had she been lied to? Had Tabarez cast her aside that quickly? Had he decided to keep El Árbol Negro? She'd heard the old cliché of how Latin people lived for the moment, but this expulsion was quicker than she'd expected. She felt anger sprouting from her back like a bouquet of hot orange flames.

Upset, she turned back to the door. If he wouldn't answer the door, she would invite herself inside. She gripped the doorknob and turned it. The slab of wood swung open easily, as though it weighed ten pounds instead of twenty times that much. Of course Tabarez had made sure that the hinges were well-oiled.

She entered the foyer and noticed a large object, wrapped in black plastic, resting immediately next to the door.

El Árbol Negro.

With her fingertips she traced its lovely branches beneath the plastic. So beautiful. She noticed a dolly sitting next to it. How thoughtful.

Remembering her host's orders, she kicked off her shoes,

then crept around the edges of the carpet. The house was completely silent.

"José Ignacio?" she shouted. "Heinrik?"

Still no response. She crept up the stairs to the second floor sitting room where she had last seen him, in his white robe, strumming his instrument.

As she rose to the landing, she caught her breath.

José Ignacio was still sitting on the sofa in the sumptuous second floor *sala*. The guitar was laying next to him. His head was tilted back, and his eyes were shut. A thin smile decorated his mouth.

Another thin smile, this one quite a bit redder, and eight inches across, decorated his throat.

José Ignacio Tabarez was not going to be dining with her this afternoon.

He was dead.

PLOTWORKS PUBLISHING

Visit Plotworks Publishing today for all these titles—and more!